Ava in Lost Pines

By Steven W. Simon

For Ian.

1

Ava was fixated on the boy in seat 28D before the engines went silent. Before the oxygen masks deployed above their heads and rebounded on their plastic tubes before settling. He had the height of the boys in her class, yet his puffy cheeks and darting eyes made her consider a younger age. His mother sat to his right, and from Ava's perspective, only her hand and three-quarters of an arm underneath a maroon sleeve were visible. She handed him sour gummy candies and defeatedly suggested that he cease leaning over the seat to stare at the passengers behind them. He ate the candies with his mouth agape and Ava could see the neon greens and reds and oranges sticking to his gapped teeth. Strands of translucent drool dripped from his bottom lip and fell onto his blue T-shirt with a yellow baseball and bat.

His eyes met hers, and he let out a high-pitched squeal as he rubbed his hands together with steady pressure. She knew then that his age was moot, for whatever days elapsed into memory, he would only reach a certain mental maturity. Whether two, three, or with luck, six, his autistic mind would find its limit and remain, no matter wrinkles nor facial hair. At least, that's what she was told, or had concluded, when they brought the 'buddies' to her fifth-grade classroom and encouraged empathy and understanding. Requirements for being a good human.

The buddies with their forced haircuts, like the boy on the plane. Ava imagined them, their fathers holding them still, and their mothers placing a bowl on their heads. Snipping around the pattern while they scream and thrash, and dirty blond and black and amber strands fall to the kitchen floor.

And on the playground, 'buddies' were replaced with 'retards,' whispered within grade school clusters on molded plastic bridges and near chain link swings.

Now, in the quiet compartment, where the jet-fueled rotations had brought comfort only moments before, the others had found their obsessions. An obese man remembered Jesus while his seatmate wilted into her arms and sobbed. A woman with a gray-black perm held her husband's hand and accepted fate without a word or a glance. Perhaps that decades-long relationship only needed something subtler.

A clean-shaven gentleman wore his suit and tie, even though the meeting wasn't until tomorrow. He was told that from the moment he left his townhouse that morning he was representing the company. He stared at his reflection through black-rimmed spectacles and sensed the razor burn as his dry-cleaned white dress shirt rubbed tight against his neck. *It would be alright*, he thought, *Mason or Dillon could be at the client site the following day was there to be any issue.*

Ava's mother held her hand and dug her nails in slightly so she'd understand that this position was to be alleviated only by her. Death, her mother thought, was a foreign thought to a child of Ava's age—at least when its arrival was palpably abrupt. Surely, the children in the pediatric cancer wards have consumed the end under fluorescent lights. At least in every moment that a man with a guitar volunteering his time isn't there or a local sports athlete isn't telling them how brave they are. Ava, her mother believed, was unprepared for death, and her daughter's actions lacked the fear that would bring her gently to heaven.

Words in a foreign language screamed repetitiously from the front. The Lord's Prayer from 7A.

7B covered his ears, he believed that the mere act of saying those words determined the worst. Hear the entire prayer—the plane breaks apart and bursts into flames. Ears covered—the plane glides smoothly through the forest of trees and comes to rest to thunderous applause of death averted. The man pushed his palms to the brink of pain against his ears.

Ava stood up and peered over the rows; the stewardess in the jump seat caught her eye and gave her a reassuring smile without showing her teeth. As quick as the smile, Ava's mother yanked her back down to her seat and tightened the seatbelts. Ava lurched to her right to spy the boy. His movements calm, eyes alert, and he was repeating something. Something short. Two words, separated by several seconds, but Ava could not make them out and her mother dug her nails into her hand and pulled her back.

There were no announcements from the cockpit. Perhaps the radios were broken, perhaps there was nothing good to say. The plane floated ethereal in the quiet that should have been there had the humans not intervened. A gradual, gentle descent towards the terrain of hills and endless firs and clearings not fit for landing, even if the aircraft could make them.

The obese man figured Jesus had heard him and slammed down the plastic window shade to ward off the outside world. He was safer with reality confined in the tube, and those in window seats slid the plastic covers down so they could be safe, too. The outliers were overruled by the brave middle-seat passengers who reached over to complete the darkened cocoon.

Silence, that odd, unexpected silence, as in a cafeteria when the entire cavernous room loses its conversation at once by happenstance. Pauses to acknowledge the oddity, then resumes. Yet here the words did not return. The prayers played on repeat in minds, sniffles had finalized the tears, and the man in 7B let go of his ears.

"Okay," uttered the boy in 28D. A beat to dart his eyes left, then above. "Bye." He held the plastic bag of sour gummy candies in his hand and when he reached in with the other, the plastic crinkled. He pulled a red and green gradient piece from the bag and slid it in his mouth, his eyes still gauging a situation beyond his comprehension. Two chews and the drool saturated the screen print on his shirt. "Okay. Bye." Crinkle. Chew. Drool. "Okay. Bye."

The flight attendant reintroduced her faux smile, her position facing the passengers made her the de facto leader of this group. Charged with reassurance in her facial expressions and she thought back to how meticulous she had been with her makeup in the hotel mirror that morning. *Had she been careful? Was there perfect symmetry and blend? Were the lines of her maroon lipstick married to the lines of her lips?* It hadn't mattered when the obese man gathered his cellulite to fit in the shrunken economy seat. Nor when the woman pulled her autistic son by a leash wrapped around her wrist and extended to the belt loop of his pants. Yet, now, she felt perfection important in the belly of a flawed, man-made vehicle as it exuded Icarus on its descent. How perfect the women seemed in the black and white photographs on the walls of the lounges she had seen at LAX, ORD, ATL, and LGA. *We are mothers to all who fly,* she thought, *and the antithesis of the ego man possesses at the design of great things they desire other men to admire.*

She had brought back her smile, and kept it as the speakers above them chirped to life. A pilot did his best to maintain a composure in his voice to the unseen cabin. She bent over and placed her hands behind her head. Business class, with its aft position, took her cue first and crunched into the demonstrated position. The ensuing rows did as their wealthier counterparts until they reached the obese man who found the position impossible, and therefore, swallowed the ends of the armrests with his imposing palms until his fingertips went white.

The boy's mother made attempted to place the boy's hands atop his head. "Okay. Okay," before he reverted to his impossible curiosity to the left, the right, and above. Ava's mother released the grip on her daughter's wrist, mimicked the others, then elbowed Ava until she too put her hands atop her head and bent over. "Okay. Bye."

Time expanded, and this bored Ava. *How can one experience life*, she thought, *in such a state of internal shadows and mechanical quiet?* So, she opened her eyes, relaxed her pose, and proffered a smile to the boy in 28D. For a moment he simply stared at her, *through her*, she thought. An expression of either deep understanding or thoughtless void, with synapses that couldn't quite connect. And when he could not determine an appropriate reaction to her facial expression, he resorted to a guttural utterance of glee. A high-pitched, prepubescent squeal as he clapped his hands once, then rubbed them to alleviate any remaining confusion.

The obese man gripped harder when he heard it. The stewardess opened her eyes and kept her gaze on the point where her black skirt met her sheer nylons. They all heard it, and they all dared not move.

The boy's mother tugged on the leash, then stopped. She had spent the last nine years worrying, chasing, hoping, praying, and considering an end. These next minutes, these were hers. She did not have an autistic son. She wanted to wake up one sunny day to find the boy who was of her gone. Disappeared. She was *her*, alone, with her hopes and wide-open pastures where she could be anything. Where every milestone her child achieves are met with jealousy over pale red wines on Friday evenings in manicured caucuses on white leather couches while men throw miniature footballs to boys in front yards. A golden retriever. Two cars in the garage and a whiteboard calendar on the refrigerator to keep them moving forwards. These next minutes were hers, and the boy was no longer there.

To Ava, the boy was *everything*. She had to understand him, right here, right now. What words would he have uttered, had the connections been made? Would he put forth reassurance that this glider would brush the trees and slow as the foliage thickened? On the smooth egress to the forest floor would be waiting the does and stags and the birds singing the song of life. Perhaps he couldn't comprehend how she could smile at a time of such peril, of such "okay, bye." How could she not know of their imminent death?

He squealed again, clapped hard twice, then rubbed his hands together. He dug his uneven fingernails into his palms until the dirt that had amassed underneath mixed with the blood he'd drawn.

The stewardess heard and understood the sound below them first. They had arrived at the treetops to where the twigs and branches scraped against the plane's underbelly and echoed through the cabin.

Ava's mother reached blindly for her daughter's head and pulled it down. The boy, whose repeated, "Okay, bye," had been whispered and uncertain rang above the scratches underneath their feet. "Okay! Bye!" and he pulled up on seatbelt clasp and thrust the two sides away from his body. His mother knew his actions without lifting her head or opening her eyes, yet did not move.

The boy stood in the aisle. "Okay!" He dug his fingers into the seatbacks as the obese man further forwards clutched the armrests and implored the boy to shut his mouth. "Bye!"

Ava raised her head and straightened her body. The plane lurched to the left and right, directed by which tree was more mature, more anchored to its roots. She stared at the wet spot where his drool had pooled on the yellow baseball bat imprinted on his shirt. "Okay!"

"Shut the fuck up!" came a command from someone whose prayer was interrupted.

"Bye!"

The stewardess thought to chastise whoever it was, but had her own prayer to consider. Besides, there was no time to determine the culprit. "Okay!"

Ava turned to her mother and watched her lips move silently.

"Bye!"

The muffled sobs returned with the realization short of acceptance.

The boy clapped his hands, pushed hard, then clapped again. Ava leaned forwards. watched the repetition, and imagined blood pouring out of his ears. With a quick flip, she was free of her seatbelt and grasped the seatbacks to propel herself as the pilots fought for an even keel. The branches, now, had become such that their presence echoed throughout the cabin and drowned out the okay and the bye. The nose of the aircraft lurched upwards until Ava's grip was left to her fingertips. Downwards and she leaped to the next row. A pull with both hands on 29C and as the plane pitched up, the boy clapped and stumbled into her arms.

She wrapped her arms around his waist and they fell backwards to the aisle floor. They sensed the acceleration as the tree trunks pulled off the wings and sliced through the tailfin. Her eyes opened and found his inches above, inspecting, searching for cues. "Okay," he whispered in the proximity.

"Okay," she whispered back and let the corners of her lips rise.

"Bye," the boy responded, matching her volume.

"Bye."

2

"Okay," Ava thought she heard. Dreamed. Imagined. Felt. "Okay," in the murkiness of her eyelids clamped. She took her first conscious gasp and the taste of chemical air released the blindness. The boy had his arm wrapped around her chest where they lay on the aisle floor. His eyes searched hers as he breathed through his mouth, not knowing if what he tasted was cause for alarm. "Okay."

There was a haze of ashen smoke that rolled through the cabin above them. An artificial heat from some unknown source. The crackles of manufactured plastics and sewn fabrics delivered the urgency to Ava at once. She sat up into the fog with her breath held and set back down on all fours to crawl towards the front of the plane where the smoke rolled out into what she imagined was penetrating daylight. After several rows, she turned back and saw that the boy had not moved.

"Okay," he said.

"Come on!"

"Okay." And he did not move. She motioned him to move forwards, and he stood up, stood still, and his features disappeared into the smoke.

"What are you doing?" she screamed, and he coughed in his new darkness. She turned herself around in the tight confines and crawled to his feet. His white shoes stained green near the toes, untied, and loose around his skinny ankles. The leash hung down between his legs, the red loop worn where held and curled on the thin carpet.

Ava reached out and grabbed it and yanked the length through his legs until she felt resistance at his groin. A panic grew in his cough and he fought her pull. "Come on!" A grating cough and a stream of saliva landed on her shoulder. She thought about praying for superhuman strength but remembered the prayers she had most recently heard—all unanswered. She reached into the heavy smoke and groped until she found his wrist and pulled him from the smoke.

He expelled the foreign inhalations, his face inches from the floor, and a puddle of drool formed.

"Okay," he told the floor, and then, gazing up, her. She stayed on his eyes for a moment to reassure and, taking the leash, led him through the economy section. Short breaks in the dense smoke let her see slumped bodies. Crooked spines bent over. Blood pooled below cracked skulls. As she moved, she listened. For struggled breaths, moaning, a call for help. She heard nothing, and she led him through the compact economy seats and when they reached first class, she knew they were the only ones alive.

The wind pushed the smoke down further in the cabin the closer they came to the freedom of daylight. Ava closed her eyes to interrupt the sting, while the boy kept his open, accepted the pain that turned his eyes crimson and constricted the blood vessels. She pulled him forwards into business class where, to their left, the metal body had separated.

Ava slid her head out of the opening, which muffled the fire's crackles as if underwater. She examined the drop to the forest floor, then reversed back into the cabin. She spied the boy, then back out, and knew that if she jumped first her last moments with him would be watching him burn alive. He'd stare down at her as his skin blistered and charred, but at last he would have no need to understand.

The image jarred her. It was one thing to imagine the horrific fates of humans on the precipice of mortality, somewhere, somehow, in some time and place. Here, now, she was confronted with its reality. To watch it unfold, and this thought pushed itself to immediacy. Peculiarly, she had crawled from her dead mother, through a sea of death, and had not even considered the implications. That is the true force of survival that supersedes all else, and under its control, she crawled behind the boy.

Ava extended her arms, pressed her hands on his butt, and drove the balls of her feet into the melting carpet to propel him forwards. His knees skittered across the floor and his body disappeared from the cabin.

She leaned out and watched his descent. He made no attempt at altering the trajectory she had set him on and landed with violence, arms outstretched onto the dirt and rotting leaves and low brush. He lay there, motionless, head down, for ten seconds or an hour. She watched him from her perch above as he came to his knees and tried to find a breath where there was none.

Her fingers gripped the edge of the broken fuselage, her legs dangled, and after a deep inhale, she released. Her feet hit first, then she fell to her side and rolled several times.

He thrust his chest out and still no air penetrated, and the leash whipped around in his struggle. She stood up, went to him, and grabbed him by the arms.

"Okay?" she asked him, and found fear returning when she realized she had never seen eyes that wide, that red, and that helpless. The guilt welled; *she* had pushed him out of the airplane. "Okay?" and he only returned an inverted gurgle. She didn't even offer the option for him to exit on his own terms. *What right did she have*, she thought, *to know what he does and doesn't know? What if he was a jumper? An excellent jumper? What if all she had to have said was 'jump,' and he would have done it?*

"Okay?" she repeated. He responded with silence, stillness, only a stare, and when she shook him desperately, he found his first breath since rising from the earth. "You're okay," she said, and pulled him in and embraced his thin frame.

"Okay," he assured her.

"Okay," she confirmed.

3

A forest. *Some* forest. An airplane carcass, burned, but recognizable. Wings somewhere back there, south of here. Engines gone, somewhere south of here. The choking smoke had transformed to silver and what was once an immediate threat diminished.

The boy approached the trees cautiously and took in the tactile responses each trunk elicited through his fingertips. The rough, patternless nature of the pine bark and the amber ants that crawled upwards, disappeared into the crevices only to reappear higher up the trunk. The smooth gray touched with olive of the beech tree. He pulled at the ashen birch bark, and when he sensed resistance, he let go.

"What's your name?" Ava asked from her seat, a log half-buried from time left alone. The boy ignored her, immersed in his new environment. "My name's Ava." He left his finger on the bark. An ant considered this new development, decided to crawl over, and continued his predetermined path up the tree. The leash rustled the dead leaves when he moved to another and touched the soft moss near the ground.

"Do you have a name?" And when he didn't respond, she continued, "Sometimes I like 'Ava,' sometimes I don't. Some of my friends call me 'Matty,' which sounds like a boy's name. I don't really care about those things. Well, I did, but I don't right now."

The boy stepped back from the trees into the small clearing, cocked his head skyward, and let out something akin to a sigh. "What's your name?" she tried again. He turned, looked at her for a moment, then walked with long strides to the airplane.

"Mom," he said to the hole they had exited, without annunciating the final 'm,' resulting in a word somewhere between 'mo' and 'ma.' "Mom," he repeated, examined his surroundings for a moment, then back to the opening. "Mom."

"Come sit down," Ava requested.

"Mom."

"What's your name?"

"Mom."

"I'm going to name you if you don't tell me."

"Mom."

"Maybe a funny name, like 'Ketchup,' or 'Monkey Butt.'"

"Mom." He jumped with the hope that he'd make it back inside the airplane, whereas his feet had barely left the ground.

"Hey 'Monkey Butt,' does that sound right?"

"Mom." Quieter.

"Hey 'Ketchup,' pass me the ketchup." She waited for him to say it again, yet he did not. "I think I'll call you 'Charlie.' That's a good sounding name. You look like a 'Charlie,' or kinda like a kid I knew named 'Charlie.' Well, his mother told our teacher that he should be called 'Charles' and then she told us, but we kept calling him 'Charlie' anyway. Didn't seem like it was mean or anything, at least not to us, and we don't think he cared."

"Mom!" he yelled up to the hole, and Ava stood quickly from the log. Each step towards him had intention, pushed the dirt down more than her seventy-pound frame should have. When she reached him, she grabbed his wrist and spun him around, away from the burned fuselage, and made sure his eyes found her.

"Your mom is dead. *My* mom is dead. Do you understand that, Charlie? We are now motherless. That fat guy, he's dead, too. That woman that told you to put on your seatbelt, she's dead. They are all dead. Do you understand?"

Charlie's eyes had lost their redness, and the dirt that had stayed on his face from his fall made the whites that much more. He smiled for a moment, either to comfort her in her mourning or to transition the conversation to the few he understood. Regardless, he wrapped his arms around her, kissed her forehead, then turned back to the airplane. "Mom."

Ava threw her arms up and then smacked them against her thighs. She grabbed the leash from behind him and pulled through the resistance when the tension reached the belt loop. Charlie stumbled back and then reasserted his posture. "Mom." She pulled again, but he didn't move.

"Get. Away," Ava commanded as she turned away from Charlie and set the leash over her shoulder, "From. The. Plane!" And she grunted as she pulled. Her body flung forwards into the ground as the stitches that had held the belt loop in place gave way.

"Mom," she heard him say, with her lips an inch from the soil, a hand still holding the leash, and pushed herself up. She sat back down on the log and ran the loop of the leash through her fingers where the red dye had worn. "Mom."

"They're going to come soon," she told him without looking up. "With the helicopters and the trucks. They'll come soon—to rescue us. Then we'll get to go home." She wrapped the leash around her wrist. "Well, you'll get to go home, I suppose. Do you have a dad?"

"Mom."

"I think I do, but I've never met him. I mean, not anytime I can remember. When I was little, I did. We're going, we *were* going to Portland to live with my aunt cause my mom lost her job. I'm scared, Charlie, well, I *was* scared, cause I don't know where we're going and I don't know who's there and I don't really know my aunt and what if I can't make any friends like the ones I had back home?"

She looked over at Charlie, his head tilted towards the breach. "Do you have any friends? Do you know what 'friends' are?" He turned and faced her, and she thought perhaps her words had found a commonality in his vocabulary, his understanding. She waited for a response, and his feet dragged along, taking twigs and leaves with him, until he set upon the log next to her.

"I can be your friend, Charlie, if you want." He picked up a stick and broke it in half, then halved the smaller piece until it was too small to reduce. "Now I'm scared for totally different reasons." As he grabbed another stick and cracked it. "Or maybe it's the same thing, cause things are still going to change now. Just differently. Everything's different for you too now, Charlie, even if you don't know it."

He threw the remaining twig to the ground, turned to her, and put his hands on her shoulders. "Thirst," he said, omitting the 't' at the end of the word.

"What?"

"Thirst."

"Oh, you're thirsty?"

"Okay."

"Okay," she confirmed, relieved that this was a request that she understood, and then realized it was one that was not easily rectified. The fire had consumed the cabin, and even if it hadn't, there was no way to get back up. "Stay here," she told him, "and listen for the helicopters."

Ava touched the side of the plane and saw how little of the machine her hand covered. The sheer scale hidden from her view back at the airport gate, through the windowless tunnel, and once inside, she was a part of its enormity. She knew that they had put her bag on the plane, or at least, she assumed they had, although she hadn't seen it happen. Someone with a nametag took it, and her guitar, from her when they first arrived at the airport. He had put stickers around the handles with her name on them, and then they disappeared.

They had to be somewhere within, and as she climbed over roots and maneuvered around trees and rounded the nose of the plane, her heart sank. She had seen the smoke above them as they crawled, but felt the fire beneath. What had become, she asked herself, of the photographs? Her friends at birthday parties. Her grandmother standing next to her grandfather, seated, holding her as a baby with the prideful expression men get when they're holding back the tears. The grainy Polaroid that she assumes is her in her father's arms, but she'd been too afraid to ask her mother what truth is in the film. Her stuffed dog, 'Doggie,' with his scars from the two-year-old wars. Friendship bracelets in a plastic freezer bag that she could match the colors to the friends. The seashell from the day they drove six hours to the beach to spend two, then turned inland to sleep in the small, familiar apartment.

Out of Charlie's sight, the tears welled up and fell down her cheeks. The reality she had suppressed in his presence, as his charge, flooded her thoughts, tripping over itself. Her mother was gone. Her friends were gone. She would never rest her head on the soothing familiarity of her bed again. She had only met her aunt once, years previously, and now that future life with her, without the transitional, buffering presence of her mother, frightened her with unknown and unlikely hypotheticals.

Guilt pushed her further from composure. Guilt of time elapsed that she had not cried, that she had suppressed the torment for what others had lost. Where had her uncontrollable agony been, why had her tears not wetted the carpet as they crawled? For her mother, most personally, but for the fat man whose fat wife will soon find her own emotional distress. For the stewardess, who with each new flight tempted the gods. Charlie's mother, and her imagined family, a husband who works in an office building cubicle on the third floor above a medical supply company, as her mother does. *Did.* Her other children who are not like Charlie.

She slumped down into the shadowy space between the plane's nose and the ground and let all the emotions, the thoughts, and the uncertainties get swallowed up by her sobs. She let them reverberate true; there was no societal norm for miles that would insist she was making a scene or being inappropriate. Only the boy, only Charlie in these lost pines, who was now, by pure luck, in her presence—a boy who knew nothing of mores. Hidden in the false cave, she had no need for thoughts or ambitions; there was only her, and she wanted to stay there for eternity.

When she finally allowed a new thought to emerge, she was not sure if it had been thirty seconds or the eternity she hoped. In school her teacher had projected a list of jobs available in adulthood, separated into *girls* and *boys*. Her side, bulleted with pink stars, listed nurse, teacher, chef, homemaker, secretary, typist, zoologist, stewardess, and waitress. The boys had their blue bullets: fireman, policeman, lawyer, doctor, astronaut, scientist, sports player, truck driver, construction worker, and many more! She walked home that day deflated and vowed to never pick up her guitar again. "Many more!" gave the boys hope, elicited options beyond what could fit on the plastic sheet projected on the wall. The omission on the *girls* side meant that those options were it, she had no hope of being Lita Ford or Joni Mitchell or Joan Jett. Grade school girls, at least here, were not meant to grow up to be famous rock guitarists. And when she reached the apartment complex door, she stopped, scanned for witnesses, and exhibited her first act of rebellion with an audible, "Fuck you, Mrs. Campbell."

In this fresh memory, Ava imagined the sound of a guitar, a single open-handed note.

She sniffled, wiped her cheeks with her sleeves, and sat up in the dirt. Another note. A third, each separated by five seconds of the forest.

She rose to her feet and inched around the nose until she could see the length of the right side of the plane. Down low, at the bottom of the plane, something had sheared through the metal, and from this opening some of the suitcases and bags had spilled out before they could be consumed. She followed the luggage path as it sloped down the terrain and wiped her eyes again. She could see Charlie in the distance, squat low, and she watched him reach out to play another note.

A navy-blue duffle bag. A maroon suitcase and a matching, smaller version. Lime-green cloth, two black wheels, and an orange string tied to the handle. Black. Gray. Blue. Luggage tags as dog tags after the battle and Ava searched for her buddy, the one whom she connected with at boot camp. They became brothers and they've made it this far and this can't be the way it ends. Black, red stripe, blue tag. Gray bottom, green top, yellow tag. Another note. Teal front and rear, red down the sides, two wheels, broken zipper in the front.

Ava dropped to her knees, ran her hand across the teal front and rear, the red down the sides, and pulled the broken zipper from right to left. She reached in and pulled out the photographs. Another note.

"Dammit," she said to herself, half-kidding as she cleared a joyful tear from her cheek and she smiled. She held the photographs against her chest to insure they were truly there, and returned them to the pocket. Another note.

"I like your song," Ava yelled to Charlie as she dragged the suitcase down to meet him. He closed the case and gently set the clasps.

He turned and looked at her. "Thirst."

"Right, you're thirsty." And Ava set about opening the luggage near them. She rummaged through the clothing, through strangers' pants, blouses, shirts, their underwear. Thought what had led someone to buy Crest toothpaste, or in other suitcases, Colgate.

She opened the navy-blue duffle bag, felt something solid wrapped in a gray sweatshirt, and pulled the clothing off what was protected. A rectangular box, concealed by wrapping paper. *John,* a tag taped to the box read, *We are so proud of you. Love, Mom and Dad.* She tore the wrapping paper, opened the box, and removed the bottle of red wine. Rummaged further and found a corkscrew, which she remembered was necessary from the bottles she had opened for her mother on those nights she invited coworkers over to speak about other coworkers.

The sun threw parallel shimmers from the west and shone spotlights on the particles floating in the air. Ava watched with curious eyes as Charlie lifted the wine bottle with both hands and let the liquid fill his mouth. She had never tasted wine, and assumed he hadn't either. His cheeks expanded, swallowed, and then let the remaining wine dribble down his chin. He set the bottle on the ground, uttered a groan, and rubbed his hands together.

"Watch your lips," she warned, remembering that her mother had warned her that wine loosened them. "We should hear the helicopters any time now," she reassured him, "or the trucks." He squealed, clapped his hands twice, then squealed again. "They'll have water for us, I'm sure, and food. I'm hungry."

She grabbed the bottle and smelled through the opening. It reminded her of a distant grape juice. She put it to her mouth, tilted until it touched her lips, then licked them. With one hand she plugged her nose and gulped it down.

"Gross," she said, and extended the bottle to him. He ignored her, stared into the trees, and giggled with his hands rubbing together at something she could not see. She imagined he was watching two deer exploring the forest floor.

"I keep having this memory, almost like a dream you can't quite remember, you know? Of me on my dad's shoulders and he walked into a truck stop and I remember the automatic doors when they opened and it feels like now, like something epic, like out of a movie. A big entrance, and I was above everything."

Charlie rubbed his head with both hands and let out a shrill scream. She imagined he saw the deer cut down by a hunter's rifle. He rose violently, unzipped the nearest suitcase, and pulled the clothing into a pile. Quickly to the next, grew the heap, and continued until he was satisfied that his construction was adequate. She watched him disappear under the clothes and listened to his frightened screams slowly dim, until they were a murmur transformed to gentle snores. She held her nose and braved another sip of wine before building her own makeshift bed. She fell to slumber with her arms wrapped tight around Doggie and the thought that *she* had saved a life, and that is one of the best things a person can do.

4

"Owls eat everything they catch," Mrs. Campbell told the class as they stood in line to collect their metal trays, "bones and all." A boy took his owl pellet in his hand, thrust it in a girl's face and she shrieked, which elicited a stern stare from their teacher.

"Now, even though they eat everything—sit down once you've gotten your tray—they can't digest everything they eat. What happens is that they regurgitate. Who remembers what 'regurgitate' means?"

"It means to throw it back up," a girl answered from the line.

"Very good, in this context, it means to bring digested food back up that has been taken in. What other animals regurgitate their food?" A boy raised his hand. "Yes, Andrew?"

"Cow's do, cause they have four stomachs."

"That's correct, Andrew."

Ava sat back down at her desk and placed the metal tray with its regurgitated ball on her desk. "It's called 'chewing their cud.'" She slid the tray until it was centered and pushed the pellet with a pencil until it too was aligned. "What other animal?" The fluorescent lights dimmed until there was only enough residual light to see the outline of the pellet and soft reflection from the corners of the metal.

"A cat," she heard, distant, an echo.

"No," with the vowel elongated.

"You've got nothing left," a confident voice shared from behind her, near the back wall or a mile from there. A trickle of rain on the window sills, four seconds, a deluge through the windows now open. A barn owl alit on the sill, turned its snowy face cocked, then another, and another.

"They've come for their babies," Ava warned. "They've come for their babies!" she repeated, now standing on her chair. "Give them back their babies!" No one heard her. The boys and girls stuck their tweezers into the soft fibrous clumps and tore them open.

"You're killing them!" A girl turned and placed her palms on Ava's desk, "send them *all* back to the mountains," and Ava wept.

"I'm so sorry," she told the first owl. "I'm so sorry," she told the second.

***

Ava's eyes flit open in her enclosure of strangers' clothing and her mind searched for a hold on her surroundings. The cool air. The blue aura that her eyes attuned to, effectuated by the yellow moon on a cloudless night. The owl's hoot that had infiltrated her dream. The potpourri of various laundry detergents. How the green sweater smelled foreign and the gray T-shirt brought her comfort, a sense of something known. "Charlie," she whispered. She waited several seconds before repeating, louder, "Charlie?" He must be a heavy sleeper, she considered. "Charlie!" And the owl responded.

She pulled the clothes from her torso, walked to Charlie's "bed," and pulled the clothing from the top. Peeled a layer, then another, and as she flung the clothes to the ground behind her, she considered the weight, the possibility that he had suffocated under a pile of strangers' clothing. That a boy, in *her* charge, was dead. Suffocated due to her lapse in responsibility, and she stopped. *It's better to have the boy be alive and dead,* she considered, *than to be dead.* In the next moment that thought was superseded by the notion that her inaction will, in the near future, cause him to be dead—and so she dug.

Ava stood over the scattered garments and chastised herself for feeling relief in his absence. She became aware that she could breathe easier, her heart no longer stuttered, awaiting the next situation she would have to rectify. She had only been with Charlie for hours, and she extrapolated that to the years his mother had endured. No, loved him? Dealt with him? All of those?

She turned west, into the blue voids between the murky shadows of the pines. North. East. South, and back to the west. She got down on her knees and studied the dirt for footprints, picked up twigs to divine a direction from a footfall, or a snap that could only be attributed to the shoe of a grade school boy. Brought to mind the detective shows she had watched with her mother in the evenings when she could not sleep. There was always a clue, something the culprit overlooked, but not here. Here was only the forest night and its antithesis to the creature comforts she had only known before she woke from the black and into the smoky airplane cabin.

Ava whistled. To the west and to the north. An owl, perhaps the same that had spoken to her before, responded. She whistled again.

Then again. The hoot came from down the hill, from where the plane had first touched down. Where the wings and the engines presumably were, and she grabbed the leash and started down to find Charlie.

***

"Okay," Charlie said as he slid down from the fallen tree that had been his perch, his shirt lifted and the bark scratched the skin on his back. He pulled his legs in, crossed them, lowered his head into his lap and shrieked as he rubbed his hands together. He knew what this was, pacing in front of him, far enough to escape yet close enough for curiosity.

He had gone there on a yellow bus once a month, in the cold months, when there was school. It was a place with cats and dogs and they showed them how to pet the animals without hurting them. "Dog," he told the fox, shrieked again, and rubbed his hands harder. The fox took a step back, unsure of the situation and unnerved by the noises. Charlie sensed the apprehension, or at least recognized that his actions had made the animal move further away. "Dog," he whispered, and put his hands on his knees with palms up to entice the fox to approach. The woman at the shelter had shown him how.

He held his breath until he couldn't, took a deep breath, then held it again. He closed his eyes and peeked through his eyelids only when he believed it was absolutely necessary.

The fox, for her part, made him earn her presence with small, calculated steps towards the boy. With every peek she inched forwards, and with every inch Charlie fought the urge to exhale a gleeful scream, to express his euphoria in this moment that overrode all others he could imagine.

He felt her wet nose slide against his fingertip, then another, and another. He opened his eyes, let out a guttural rumble that soon reached a high-pitched yelp, and the fox scurried away into the brush.

"Okay," Charlie said, apologizing, and his eyes strained to convey the message that he will not let that happen again. He reset his pose, set his fingers out further, and waited. This time he did not peek, and when he sensed the fox's breath on his fingertips, he opened his eyes cautiously.

The fox took her time, but was always ready for an expeditious retreat. Charlie reached his hand out to touch her head and she backed away. Undeterred, he put his hand back and waited for her next move. She returned, sniffed his shoes, and explored his shoelace with her teeth. Charlie smiled, let a murmur escape, and the animal met his eyes with hers.

She backed up, cocked her red-orange head, and leaped to the fallen tree that supported Charlie's back. "Dog," he said as he turned his head to her, and she responded with perked ears. Again, he extended an arm to her, and again she inhaled his scent. Her tongue flit against his coarse, uneven fingernails. "Dog," he told her, as the sensation elicited a subtle grin.

And then, abruptly, she pulled her head from his open palm and studied the woods with ears honed. Charlie kept his position, his eyes stayed, and he hoped that his stare could compel her to lick his skin again, yet her attention was not to be regained. "Dog. Okay," he conceded and set his fingers to drawing circles in the dirt.

He looked over his shoulder to see if the fox was still there. She was, and when he turned his head back, there, in the distant darkness, he saw an amber hue floating in the distant darkness, slowly drawing closer.

***

Ava set a brisk pace through the trees and followed the flattened path where the plane had slid across the ground. Amid the blue tinge under the stalking moon, she stepped over and around the metal carnage that littered her route. Each a new reminder of what they had endured, and brought to her mind an image of the terror. Each separated by a dark, empty space that intensified the former and the latter. "Keep breathing," she told herself aloud, "don't lose your nerve."

Internally, she chastised herself for not reattaching the leash when she had the chance. When she heard his nasally snores. Had she done that, and crawled into his heap, they would still be asleep, waiting for the men in uniforms to take them somewhere, somewhere safe.

She clenched the leash in her hand to push aside the thoughts, the embarrassment. "Stupid," she said. "It's okay, it'll be okay," and a scream shook her into the present, ahead of her, and she hastened her pace in its direction.

What if I yelled out for him, she asked herself? But what would I yell, the name I'd given him? Would he come to me? Would he run? Hide? She heard him again and adjusted her heading slightly to the left where the forest thickened.

Her ears were alert for any perceptible clue that would guide her to him without informing him of her presence. When she was close, he refrained from any additional utterance, and as she parted her lips to speak his name, she saw something foreign in her peripheral vision. Her body slunk down behind a tree trunk and she cautiously pulled herself around the bark.

The large figure plodded slowly through the trees with a lantern of warm yellow held in an outstretched hand. It moved, and she watched it move from her right to her left. It moved, and when it stopped, she held still, unsure if it could hear her living. It moved, and she exhaled, and she wondered if she held her breath again if it could hear her heartbeat. It stopped, and the light from the lantern lowered.

She wished for her owl to hoot, anything to break the silence in those moments. Anything to know what this *thing* was and to know Charlie was safe. She watched the shadow move behind the lantern but could not discern its actions from her position—close enough to perceive danger but far enough not to know what that danger was. She caught herself holding her breath, told her heart to quiet, and as the echo of the gunshot still rang, she flung herself to the ground. At first, she knew she was dead and then she knew that she was not. "Charlie," she whispered into the leaves and twigs and dirt and the tears that fell uncontrollably. "Charlie."

5

"Dog?" Charlie asked, after the gunshot. There had been an interruption—the silence, a noise, then a return to quiet. He stood, pushed an audible string of syllables towards the hovering lantern, turned and set his hands on the fallen tree and searched for the fox. He climbed up and settled into a perched position, his knees nestled into his armpits.

"Dog," he told the creature prone in the brush that had sprouted from the decaying nutrients. He slid gingerly down the arc of the tree and perched again, this time over the fox. Her mouth opened slightly with labored breaths. He picked her up, held her against his chest, and a warmth saturated his shirt. "Dog," he repeated, and kept watch on her breaths until the second interruption illuminated the immediate forest around him.

"Dog," he offered the figure standing before him, and extended the fox as his eyes were forced to quickly adjust to the new yellow radiance he found himself within. Charlie's mind was built to key on facial expressions, and this figure had his hidden. This was something that he had never dealt with, it stifled his fight or flight response. He stared as the man took the fox with a gentle hand and put it in a satchel bag that hung from his side, slung over his shoulder.

His hair was wild and long, each black strand bunched with others, intermingled with the grays, and parted to reveal only a triangle of skin at his forehead. His eyes were partially hidden by wayward hairs, his beard on par, and kept his lips a secret. A torso covered in layers of patchwork apparel that mixed leathers with dirtied cottons to cover his considerable frame. The rifle in his left hand, and the fox let death come in his right.

There was the same mismatched attire from his waist on down, ending at heavy boots which were laced tight and double-knotted. Charlie stared at the boots, accumulated all the knowledge he could ascertain from them, and lifted his head back up to meet what little of the man's eyes he could.

"Okay," Charlie whispered. The new figure cocked his head slightly. "Okay," Charlie suggested again, this time with more force.

The man blinked, held the darkness for a moment, then shot his eyes open. "Okay." And the man slung the rifle from his side, and the butt slammed into the side of Charlie's head. In an instant the boy was flat and immobile on the forest floor.

***

Ava watched as the man scooped Charlie from the ground and flung him over his shoulder. It's a man, she convinced herself, as no *woman* would do that. Charlie's limp body bounced against his back as he carried him back in the direction from where he first appeared. There was a rage within as she followed the light, one she had never felt before—at least not one that matched the degree. She stalked from a distance with little regard for her footfalls. She hoped he would hear her, she imagined how she would kill this man. Bashing his head in with his own rifle. Stabbing his neck with a knife and watching the blood spurt out as he gasped. Jumping on his back and choking him until his body lay still. And then, the lantern ceased its progress and lifted higher. He had heard something; he had heard *her*.

She threw herself to the ground, closed her eyes, and tried to remember the prayer she'd heard on the airplane as she knew none. Held her biceps with opposing hands and felt for muscles but found none. Her rage would be nothing to overcome this man, this beast. There was no ability in her petite frame to take his rifle. Had she a knife, there would be no strength to plunge it into an artery, and no pressure to deny his brain circulation. Thus, she waited, positioned to watch the lantern's movements, and when it resumed its path from left to right, she followed again.

The night had no intention of expiring, every step she took lasted an hour, and every pause, two. The plane, the fire, their escape, it all seemed so distant in the immediacy of the threat. All her wants and desires fell from her consciousness and were buried, tamped down into the earth. The man paused in a clearing of tree stumps while he cautiously circled with the lamp and listened through the pines before disappearing into the cabin.

Ava made her way to the structure, tree by tree, still unsure of the creature's abilities, and when near enough, she ran her hands along the craggy logs that made up its bulk. A small window was set on the short end of the cabin and cloth hung from inside to block her view. A pile of firewood was stacked near her feet and she grabbed the ax by its handle set against the cabin. The rage she had earlier reemerged, then quickly dissipated as she struggled to handle the weapon, and she set it back in its place.

The rear was made entirely of the logs hewn from what could be construed as the front yard. The opposing narrow side had the same window, yet it wasn't placed even to its counterpart. She kept her ears alert as she came around to the front of the cabin. *It was odd*, she thought, *that there were no windows.* Maybe it was for safety, maybe he didn't have the money for the glass. Maybe he has a wife inside and she had asked that there be no windows in the front. She felt the heft of the door but did not press, lest she elicit a squeak from its hinges. She let her hand fall, retreated to a stump and sat, unsure of what to do next.

6

The man set the limp fox on a small table and slit through her belly with a knife. Each ensuing cut was precise as he skinned the animal, removed the organs, and organized the meat on the table, leaving bloody streaks on the wood.

He worked in silence, folded a frayed towel and used it to protect his hand from the heat of the iron stove as he fed wood into its belly. He set a timer in his mind as the heat crackled the new tinder, and in the interim he turned and watched Charlie snore.

He was aware that his decision to live in solitary seclusion had created a patchwork existence, both in his mind and in his surroundings. He had given up on determining which memories were true and which were the result of years lacking socialization. Of years left to his mind without the security of second opinions. This life chosen had manifested into the physical, be it his random attire or the cot layered in furs sewn together from whatever animals he had hunted successfully. He studied the boy, pulled into a fetal position, snoring on his cot. His young features, his fragility, the bruise on his temple from where he had struck him. The man, had he no beard, would have exposed his embarrassment with reddened cheeks for the lapse in judgment, and he set the meat on the stove to feed the boy in an act of attrition.

"Okay," Charlie muttered, still prone, with his pupils dancing to perceive the room dimly lit by the lantern. He picked at the different furs under his body and paused with each tactile difference. "Okay," he projected to the man as he sat up on the cot. The man turned his frame to face the boy, and the two stared without words while the meat cooked. "Okay," Charlie suggested again.

The man pulled in an extended breath through his nostril and on the exhale proffered his response, "Okay." Charlie deliberated on the word, its tone, its volume, and the harshness of the consonant.

"Okay," the boy responded once satisfied.

"Okay," the man said as he smiled and quickly retracted the emotion. He hoped that it was the absurdity of the interaction that brought the reaction and not something resembling kinship.

Charlie pressed his palm against his bruised head and stood from the cot. The man stayed seated, observed, and showed no indication that he would interrupt the boy. Charlie knelt to feel the furs again. Reached up and pulled a curtain away from the window pane. Sat down, pulled open the flap of a cardboard box, and looked at the man to reassure or dissuade him from further investigation.

The man nodded slowly, once, and when Charlie was satisfied that an aggressive action was not forthcoming, he picked through the contents stored in a cardboard box. A small knife wrapped in a sheet of sandpaper that upset his fingertips. A bird, a dog, a cat, an elephant, all carved from wood and smoothed to where the sensation made Charlie grin and caused a drop of saliva to darken the elephant's back from birch to walnut. He set each on the floor to make a row of animals.

"I saw an elephant once," the man said, then cleared his throat, "not at a zoo, but in the wild." Charlie took a photograph from the box, studied the images of people he did not know, ran the soft edges underneath his fingernails, then put the wrinkled rectangular next to the animals.

Charlie kept his focus on the next photograph as the man tended to the fox meat on the stove. He felt the corners under his fingernails, investigated, then placed it atop the former on the floor. The man stuck a metal prong into the pieces of fox meat, transferred them to a wooden board, then set the board on the table.

The box emptied, Charlie touched each wooden animal with his index finger. He aligned the edges of the photographs to neaten the pile and stared at the knife and sandpaper, wishing that they did not exist.

"Thir," Charlie said quietly as he sprung quickly from the floor. When the man didn't respond, he stepped closer. "Thir," he repeated, louder. The man had heard him this time, yet didn't move. The steam that lifted into the air from the cooling meat took Charlie's attention, which quickly dissipated. "Thir," he pressed again, this time with his face close for emphasis.

The man did not understand the word. The welt on Charlie's temple, the reds and the blues and the browns, especially clear in this proximity, added to his embarrassment, and he chose not to respond. Charlie opened his mouth to utter once more, but instead inhaled, then brought his lips back together.

Charlie looked away and scratched his chest. He stepped back to the cardboard box, smiled awkwardly, and struck his forehead with the palm of his hand. He screamed a noise that sounded like, "Ya," with the vowel stretched and as it continued his pitch raised. He hit himself several times while he repeated, "Ya," then jumped onto the cot and sat with his legs crossed. Bent his head into his lap, which exposed the ridges of his spine. He growled, and each growl commenced with a low register and peaked in a piercing high. He rose, slapped his kneecaps, dug his fingernails in, buried his head, then lifted again.

The man reluctantly brought back memories of his own children, thoughts he had pushed down into the deep recesses, to help him facilitate a resolution. Before he walked into the forest and built the cabin. Before he had abandoned society and denied the world.

Each thought recovered and flickered into imagery, their accompanying audio distant, and the scenes in his head skipped around as the boy screamed. Nothing coherent coalesced, all he knew was that they hated him, and they had every right to hate him. This cabin was not his refuge, it never was, it was his self-made prison, and he stood up in his cell and drew his fingers in to make a fist. He had quieted the boy before, and he knew he could do it again.

He stood up and took a step towards Charlie, then another. Charlie was oblivious to the approaching violence, and in between his howls, the wood in the stove cracked and sizzled. On the third step the man stopped, Charlie's screams flipped to soft *muhs* and their eyes went to the door as it vibrated on its hinges.

Ava stepped back from the door, steadied herself, and lunged again. Her petite body moved the wood slightly as her shoulder connected, and again she rammed. When her efforts fell short, she pounded with her fists and kicked at the door with the soles of her shoes.

"Let me in!" she demanded. "Don't you touch him!"

Charlie stared at the man for reassurance, but the man kept watching the door, parsing the situation and he searched his mind for a decision. The exterior clamor that echoed inside ceased, but it was only for a moment as Ava recovered, and it returned with additional force. Her voice crackled as she again demanded entrance.

There was a hesitancy in the man's movement to the door. The cues; a girl's voice, her inability to breach the door. The weak sounds that her fists produced against the wood, each converged to calm his mind, to put him in a position of control. And yet, it was his confidence, his hubris, that had been his downfall in the years past. His decisions, his thoughts, and his actions, those were the reasons he was in this cabin with a strange boy and an irate girl at the door. They were the reason he took no interest in his hair and let it hide his eyes. The reason he lost all faith in his words, his convictions, and left him to live among the deer and the fox and the insects.

Under Charlie's curious eyes, the man lifted the latch that had foiled Ava's attempts, and pulled the door open only the inches that were necessary for his eyes to survey. He peered out at his level, then kept bending his neck down until he finally saw her figure.

A young girl, nine, maybe ten years old, he presumed. Her hair was brown, more towards black than blond, and pulled back in a ponytail. Eyes wide, and freckles on her cheeks. A dirtied shirt, purple and white stripes. Her light blue jeans and black canvas shoes. A red leash clasped in her hand. He compared her features to his own daughter at that age, then pulled his eyes shut to separate the thought from his mind.

Ava said nothing, for she had already said what was needed. It was on the man to say something now, to *do* something now. He didn't resemble her father in the photograph. *Had he*, she thought, *perhaps he would have some benefit of her doubt.* His features revealed to her more a sinner than a saint. A devil in a forest cabin where the floorboards would turn to sand and pull them down into the fiery earth and swallow them whole into the depths of hell. His features were, by design, a message of shadows, the antithesis of social acceptability, and they worked wonders through the opening in the view of a child. She craned her neck and met the devil in his eye. Only death, she concluded, would stop her from entering the cabin, and that wouldn't be the *worst* thing. She set her fists against the door and pushed. The man resisted without much effort. Then, with a slow inhale, he queried his mind for a decision, and on the exhale, released his grip from the door.

7

Ava stood between the man near the table and the cooling fox meat, Charlie sat on the cot. She eyed the man, then turned to Charlie, who sat calmly on the furs. The cabin's warmth led her to rub her shoulders with her opposing hands, realizing only now that she had been cold. She saw the meat and perceived her hunger. The cardboard box. Animal figurines carved from wood. The photographs. A pot and a pan hung from nails. Tin cups with distinct dents.

Charlie vocalized a noise that sought to be a word, but didn't quite make it. The noise startled both Ava and the man, both of whom had been satisfied in the interim silence accented by the stove.

A small chest was next to the cot, and Ava wondered what contents were hidden inside. The rifle laid against a wall. Apples and berries in glass jars on a shelf. A small pile of firewood on the floor next to the stove. Four plates of different designs.

Charlie spoke again; the man heard, "Thir," and Ava, "Thirs."

"He said that before," the man told her, "I don't know what it means."

"He's saying 'thirsty,'" she explained without turning to him, "he's thirsty." And she recognized her own thirst.

"Hmmm," the man murmured as Ava sat down on the cot next to Charlie. The man pulled the table several feet towards the cot. He got down on his knees, pried three floorboards from their places, and set them aside. There, within the rectangular hole dug in the earth below the cabin's floor, was an olive-green duffle bag. A name had been printed along its side in black, block letters, but was unrecognizable.

The man unzipped the bag, and the guilt returned. *He was not a bad man*, he thought, *not evil, at least*. He rued the mistakes he had made, which comforted him in the knowledge that psychopathy could not be pinned on him. Yet, here was proof that he was a thief. Not only that, but proof that he was not a *true* survivalist. He *earned* this, he rationalized, through the twenty-five-mile trek that it took to get to the general store. His ability to enter and exit unseen, to retreat to the woods. This was all needed for survival, he reminded himself, as he moved the pornographic magazine to the bottom of the bag. Lantern oil, the bullets, gauzes and bandages of varying sizes. Aspirin, heartburn chews, toothpaste and a toothbrush. Cans of vegetables, fruit cocktail, a can of condensed milk. All evidence if he's to be caught, all hidden out of sight. When he had retrieved the items, he zipped the bag, set the floorboards back in place, and moved the table back to its original position.

"C'mon," he said to the children, and motioned for them to join him around the table. He put the glass bottles of Coca-Cola on the table and popped the caps with an opener. *This man*, Ava thought, *could have bloody fangs and horns, and she would still go to that table to satisfy her thirst.* She took Charlie's hand, led him to the table, and reassured him as the man handed him a bottle.

They watched as Charlie covered the opening with his mouth and he swallowed quickly to match the speed at which the soda left the bottle. He coughed the liquid that entered his lungs, smiled, and uttered his approval as it dribbled down his chin. Ava took several sips and set the bottle down on the table.

The man put three plates on the table and portioned the meat. Charlie sat down on the lone chair, and they bit into the fox. The man chewed thoroughly, knowing the toughness of the game meat, and Ava adjusted after the first bite. Charlie only knew soft foods, gummy candies, PB&J sandwiches, pizza, and so Ava took the role of slapping his back when he tried to swallow prematurely.

"Didn't you hear it?" Ava asked the man.

"Hear what?"

"The plane crash."

"I heard something."

"It had to have been loud."

"Hmm."

"And you don't even, you weren't even curious?"

"It was none of my business."

"Where do you think we've come from?"

"None of my business."

"You think we just appeared here, out of nowhere?"

The man thought to respond, but it would be the same response. "Did you lose your dog?" he asked, glancing at the leash still in her hand.

"Charlie is *not* a dog," she chastised him.

He moved his gaze to the boy and realized that the leash was for the boy. "You shouldn't put a leash on a person," he told her as she hit Charlie's back. "Lest he's a prisoner, then it's okay."

"Well, if I did have this leash on him, we wouldn't be here right now, he wouldn't have run off."

"Would that have been a good thing?"

"Well, the helicopters are probably there and we'd get to go"—she paused—"home."

"I'll get you to the road, from there you can find your way."

Ava imagined some unseen road. "No, we need to get back to the plane."

"Are you sure there's a plane?"

"Of *course*, there's a plane," she quickly shot back at the absurd question. "How do you think we got here?"

The man recollected the noise he had heard. It could have been anything: a plane crashing through the trees, bears chasing, elk fighting, a tree whose time had come. Memory, he had learned, was not to be trusted, even when it was fresh and wet with dew.

"I can get you to the road."

Ava slapped Charlie's back to relieve the obstruction in his throat without averting her eyes from the man. The boy uttered something nonsensical and, satisfied with his opinion, ripped another piece of meat with his teeth.

Defeated, she ended the discussion. *He would be more likely to be swayed*, she strategized, *when they were outside.* A leashed Charlie would give her the advantage of numbers to his objection.

The interlude brought arousal to her other senses. The squishy sound of the meat as his gapped teeth bit down while he breathed through his mouth. How his drool paused at the tip of his chin before dropping onto his lap. The dust and dankness that reminded her of her grandmother's attic with the discarded furniture and clothes that meant something to someone at some time. The muskiness of the man, how the dirt from his attire had become a part of him and fused with the salty sweat that he'd let dry on his skin. She scratched her head as she imagined what infestations might have found a home on his head. She took a sip of her Coke in an attempt to change the subject.

Instead, her mind sketched her in her bed, her mother pulling the blanket over her shoulders and the warmth became real. It built a montage of safety in her father's arms and how he let her go to take her first steps as a child—a memory none of us remember. Yet she sensed his squeeze and the confidence he gave her was real, there, in that cabin. *It was her responsibility*, she thought as she turned towards the boy, *he* was her responsibility—

and that frightened her beyond any courage her mind could conjure.

Charlie held the bones over his plate. He studied them, then set them down gently in either reverence to the deceased animal or he simply didn't like the sound they would make against the ceramic. He looked at the man, then Ava, then surveyed the room. Back to Ava, then the man, and he stood up from the chair.

"Pot," the man heard Charlie say, as he watched him pivot his feet to see the entirety of the cabin. The man turned to Ava for clarification.

"Potty," Ava heard.

"He has to go to the bathroom," she told him confidently. "I think," she added, realizing that she had no idea.

Charlie looked at the man, then walked over to Ava. She took a step back as he reached out and grasped her shirt sleeve gently. With two fingers he pulled her towards him, "Potty," he repeated.

"So go to the bathroom," she instructed him, "go 'potty.'"

He cocked his head as he tugged again. "Potty."

"Out back," the man said, as Ava realized that the one-room cabin was just that, one room. "About two hundred feet off the back of the cabin." He took a red flashlight from a shelf, checked if it worked, then handed it to her.

She didn't want to take him. How disgusting is this bathroom in the woods? One that *that* man uses? What if Charlie insisted she stay with him as he did his business? She didn't want to be that intimate with him. She stared at the man, then at Charlie, and imagined seeing his privates. She did not want to take him, but he was her responsibility.

"Out back," he repeated. "About two hundred feet off."

***

Ava fixed the flashlight beam on the outhouse door. A wooden edifice, not old, although weathered. A crescent moon was cut out near the top of the door, as that is what the Western's told us should be done. She opened the door slightly, braced for the odorous nature to seep into her nostrils, yet found the foulness muted by another smell. *Vanilla*, she thought. *No, laundry.*

She pulled the door wide, stepped inside, and found herself in an oasis of bare wood carved into a working sink, with hoses running to somewhere. Rolls of toilet paper set on a small, vertical shelf. A porcelain seat drilled into an octagonal base of wooden slats. Hand soap. A small towel. Air fresheners doing their best to overcome the undeniable aroma that this was a place of business.

"Potty," Charlie said, still outside.

"Oh, sorry," she apologized, set the flashlight on the sink for some light, and then let him in. He made no indication that he needed her assistance. "I'm going after you."

He exited, she entered, then she exited and the lavender scent of the hand soap followed her. "Dog," Charlie said into the empty woods, and she grasped his wrist. She had decided in the privacy of the privy that the man was of no use to them. The road was no good. They were coming, with the helicopters and the dogs trained to sniff out the survivors.

"Come on," she urged as she pulled.

"Dog."

"Let's go."

"Dog."

"We have to get back to the plane."

Charlie turned his body to survey more of the forest and let his arm stay held behind his back.

"Let's go." She dug her heels into the ground, he lurched forwards, then regained his balance. "You stupid boy," she scolded, and immediately regretted the insult. "We have to go."

"Dog," he whispered.

"Yes," she echoed, and she released her grip to relieve the ache in her hand. "Yes," she said, "let's go find dog. Let's go find your dog."

He turned to her, slapped his palms onto her shoulders and dug in. "Dog."

"Yes," Ava confirmed while he neglected to blink in his stare. "Let's go find dog."

She took steps towards the cabin, quickened to a jog, and turned her head to see Charlie following the flashlight beams. Faster, and he kept pace. Past the cabin. Up a hill. Down through a ravine, and next to a small stream, Ava stopped.

"Dog," Charlie said through hard gasps, and stopped a few feet from her. Ava pushed her arm out to extend the reach of the flashlight and turned in a circle.

"Charlie," she whispered. "Do you know how to get back?"

His breathing normalized, but he didn't respond. "Back to the airplane, I mean." He sat down on the ground, picked up a crisp leaf and inspected its form.

"I don't remember which way I came to find you," she said, embarrassed. "Charlie?"

He ripped the leaf into strips, then picked up another. A bird awoke somewhere in the canopy of trees. Then another, until the entire avian community was aware of the slight dawn in the eastern sky. "Dog?" Charlie asked the birds, as if they had an answer.

"Come on," Ava said to him as she lowered her free hand to him. He looked up at her, began to say something, then didn't. "Come on, Charlie," she urged, "let's go."

It was the birds that had awoken her in the pre-dawn hours. Or, perhaps, it was her mother who had, and the tweets were the first sounds that her conscious recognized. In either case, her mind had, in these woods, brought to the forefront the memory of her mother sobbing at the kitchen table. How she offered her stuffed dog to comfort her and how her mother held her. How she told her everything was going to be alright.

Charlie took her hand, and sprung to his feet. He stared at her eyes, cocked his head, and wiped a tear from her cheek. "Okay," he told her.

Ava sniffled and wiped the others. "Okay, Charlie," she said with an unconscious smile. "Okay."

She led him back the way they had come. Towards the smell of burning firewood and the nicely appointed bathroom far from civilization. Back to the man who offered guidance and in turn they had abandoned him. As they walked, her adrenaline gave way to exhaustion. Her curiosity grew as to the rescue operation. *They had been in a plane crash, right? Her mother was dead, right?* She imagined it was all a dream and she would wake up at any moment. She tried to will herself to wake up, to gasp awareness from her pillow. In her bed, in her house. Yet they were moving, there was no bed that she knew, no images of a house she had never seen. And when the cabin came into view, she knew it was not a dream. This was *real*, at least this part, and the sun broke through the horizon to make the forest air a muted gray.

8

The man was sitting on a tree stump in front of the cabin door when Ava and Charlie appeared in the trees and approached. He had expected her to run. He would have. He had taken the time to prepare for their trek to the road, packed a rucksack with jerked meat, trail mix, and water. He held the rifle strap in one hand, the gun slung over his shoulder, and the red leash in his other hand. He had expected her to return, he had become accustomed to these woods, but knew that the uninitiated are lost within the trees until they acquiesce to nature's supremacy. One must wander without a destination, effortless, in the pines, only then had he understood the clandestine paths and how to survive the seasons.

"Is he a dog," the man asked Ava as he extended the leash, "or a boy?"

She sneered at him and snatched the leash from his hand. "He," she started as she walked to Charlie pulling the bark from a tree, "is a boy."

Charlie didn't react as she clipped the leash to his belt loop. "A boy isn't supposed to be leashed."

"Yeah, well, I don't want him running away." She walked towards the man, Charlie accepted the pull of the leash and followed her. "Let's go."

"Hmm."

"You said you'd take us to the road."

"That I did." He remained seated on the stump.

"So"—she leaned in—"let's go."

He stood with a grunt, adjusted the gun and rucksack. "Let's."

Ava waited until he had determined a direction and set off twenty paces ahead. She was still leery of the man, yet there was no one else to trust. "North," she whispered to herself after her first steps. "The sun is to our right." Charlie's body resisted the leash for a moment, then he obeyed.

They walked in silence for hours. She was unsure how many had elapsed when the man sat down on a fallen trunk and offered them each a bottle of water. The sun had risen in the sky, but was still not above them.

"Hungry?" he asked Ava.

"No, thank you," she replied, having forgotten her disdain.

He extended a bag of trail mix to Charlie, who ripped open the plastic bag. He carefully picked a piece of chocolate and placed it deep between his molars. Ava watched him, captivated by the drool she could control, and took notice of the teeth marks left on his finger. He turned his head and stared into her eyes, again searching, and she averted her gaze.

Where was the plane? she asked herself. *This did happen, it was too real not to happen. I'm going crazy. I'm not crazy. I'm too young to be crazy. But Charlie is crazy. That's different. He was born crazy. His brain doesn't work right. But where was the rescue? Why did only us survive? Why didn't I survive with someone normal, someone who could tell me if this was a dream or if this is real? Where were the news helicopters that take the video of the smoking wreckage? It doesn't make sense, and damn that boy that can't make it make sense.* She turned quickly to reengage Charlie. *Damn this stupid boy who won't tell me anything except 'thirsty' and 'dog' and 'hungry.' Can't he say 'plane crash,' is that so hard?*

"Let's go," the man directed as he stood up.

"C'mon, Charlie," she said and gently pulled on the leash. Again, she waited for the man to be a good ways ahead of them before her first step. "North, still."

As they walked, she tried to set reminders of their pathless journey. An odd-looking branch. Two branches that had fallen and formed a cross on the ground. The dead tree with no leaves. With every new landmark she committed to memory, she forgot two, and gave up the activity. She wondered how many landmarks the man had set aside in his mind and how he recalled them when needed.

"I don't know your name," she blurted out when the silence became too much. The man stopped walking, startled by the intrusion and the nature of the question.

"Is it important?" he asked and returned to his steady pace.

"Of course, it is," she retorted, and sped up to cut their distance.

"If it was important, you would have asked me when you met me."

"When I met you, I thought you were hurting my friend."

"And after that?"

"I didn't think about it."

"You should have."

"Hey!" She was almost parallel to him, with Charlie still in tow. "I just survived a plane crash! You tell me you'd have your brain working right after something like that."

The man stopped. "It's not important."

"Why? Why isn't it important?"

"It's just not."

"Why?"

He stepped towards her. "Because once we reach the road, we will never see each other again."

"That's no reason."

"It is to me," and he resumed walking.

"Okay, fine," she said, keeping up with him. "I named Charlie, so I can name you."

"Fine by me."

"Tommy. No, Mister Tommy. No, that sounds dumb. You aren't a 'Tommy.' Paul? Jimmy? Jimmy is my neighbor, he's dirty and eats raw hot dogs without a shirt in his driveway. You're dirty, do you eat raw hot dogs?" The man didn't answer. "You're wearing a shirt, lots of them. Matt, Matthew? I don't know. Wait, Jimmy *was* my neighbor."

Ava had tried to keep the memories at bay, but her naming game had let one slip through. The man stopped and studied the position of the sun. She mimicked, but lacked the knowledge of the distance that remained. When they resumed the trek, their pace accelerated, and Ava's grip tightened on the leash, pulling Charlie along until he acclimated to the new speed.

Boredom returned, and she imagined peril in the trees. *A wandering band of backwoods hillbillies in denim overalls, keen to protect their territory. A hidden booby trap flung the man up into a net, suspended by a tree. He threw a hidden handgun to her, and she took them out, one by one, between their eyes above their rotted and missing teeth.*

A mountain lion that pounced on Charlie's back. How she wrestled it, tamed it, and now it was a part of their pack. She named it 'Willa,' and now it was the lion that took out the hillbillies.

Charlie shot in the head by a wayward hunter, but instead of killing him, it made him normal. He explained to the man that there was a plane crash and that Ava had saved his life. The man knelt, held them tightly in his arms, and sobbed as he apologized for not believing her.

Resistance on the leash pulled her from her daydreams. "Come on," she instructed Charlie, who stood still. His lips came together and parted as he gazed without focus. His lips again, and Ava waited for the word—or part of a word, to be vocalized.

She turned and saw that the man continued, unaware that they had stopped. "Come on," she repeated.

"Oh, gross!" She covered her eyes as Charlie pulled his pants down to his ankles and urinated on the forest floor. "Tell me when you're done," and she immediately realized the folly of her request. With shut eyes, she waited until she was almost positive he was finished.

"Gross," she reiterated, as she caught a glimpse of his pale, bare bottom before his pants were at his waist.

"Okay," he told her, with that stare. Unsettled, she broke the connection and set them to a jog to catch up with the man.

On her mind went. Between brambles. Over fallen branches. A left detour to avoid a decaying deer feasted upon by gnats and flies. To the right to avoid a stagnant pond slimy with algae. The sun was in its descent, now below the canopy, and cast sparkled light through the forest.

It wasn't a sight that stopped her, and with Charlie's eyes everywhere but forwards, he pushed into her. She stumbled for a moment and then regained her balance.

"Okay," he said, apologetically.

"Hush," she commanded.

"Okay."

No, it was a sound. A barely audible rumble that seemed to be getting louder.

"Okay," he said again, and she covered his mouth with her hand.

The sound grew closer. A symphony of mechanical grunts and the waves of decibels between gears. She stood still, her hand kept over his mouth until she was sure.

"Charlie," she said to him while trying to see beyond the trees. "That's a truck. That is civilization."

The man had maintained his gait, so she sprinted through the woods after him as she yanked Charlie along. The sound of the truck went from there left and disappeared some seconds later to their right. They walked in single file, and each fell into darkness when they passed a tree that cut off the remaining sunlight.

She saw the white light and was drawn to it. Excited to be near it as it illuminated the signs taped to the general store window. *Twenty-four packs of Budweiser. Oscar Mayer deli meat. Mailing services. Save one dollar on any Marlboro. Bait here.*

"There you go," the man told them. "The road."

Ava stared down the expanse that stretched eternally to her left, and then to her right. All that remained of the day was a pinkish hue at the horizon. A rusted light pole in the store parking lot buzzed, then the other, and the gravel was bathed in artificial orange.

"But where do we go?" she asked, staring at the store. "Which way do we go?"

When the gruff voice she'd come to rely on didn't respond, she slowly turned around to the trees. He was gone.

"Mister!" she yelled. "Sir!"

Ava sat down on the grassy shoulder of the road. *Just me and Charlie, again. If it's only been a day, why does it feel like this has been going on forever? What the hell was wrong with that man?*

"Don't you know we need help!" she screamed into the trees. "Getting us to a road when we don't know where we are isn't *help*! It's stupid! Like a mean trick!"

She pulled at the blades of grass and a tear fell to her hand before she knew her emotions. "My mom is gone, Charlie. Your mom is gone." She looked at him, and then at the sky. "Where are the stupid helicopters! You're supposed to rescue us!"

Charlie stepped to her, sat down, and put his arm around her.

"Okay."

"It's not okay, Charlie. None of this makes any sense and we're no closer to getting home and I don't even have a home and I just," she paused and examined him. "I just really want to go home. I want to be clean, in pajamas, under my covers and listening to my alarm clock that is next to my bed and hear it make that click to the next minute. I want to hear the TV in the other room. I want my belly full and I... I just want my mom."

"Okay."

"It's not okay, Charlie." And she turned away, ashamed of how much she had shared.

"Okay."

"It's not, it's really not." She peered at him again, and the parking lot lights cast enough ambience that she could see tears falling from his eyes.

"You don't," she began as she wiped away his tears, "you don't even know why you're crying do you?"

Charlie didn't respond. After a few minutes he stood and grasped her arm to pull her up from the ground.

"Thirs," he informed her.

"Okay, Charlie," she said. "Okay."

9

Ava chose to walk west down the deserted road, towards the dwindling light. She muttered her disdain to the day, Sunday, as they walked the gravel shoulder that bordered the endless pavement. *Had it been any other day, the man in the store would have called for help. He would have taken them in with his inborn kindness. Fed them. Given them juice and told them everything would be alright. Had the pay phone worked, they would be sitting on the concrete blocks that marked the parking spaces. They would be waiting for the police officers to put their hands on their shoulders and tell them everything would be alright.*

Charlie followed behind her, close enough so the leash was not taut, yet sufficiently far to be forgotten as she daydreamed. His needs satisfied in the present, he made no requests.

As the darkness overtook them and the crickets quieted in the brush, his mind relaxed, as there was nothing left to understand.

She led them, for there was nothing else for her. For them. A mile or ten in the thick rural darkness. In the quiet, interrupted only by the crunch of the rocks beneath their feet that guided them.

Three miles, then another, and Ava stopped suddenly. Charlie, awash in his immediate existence, recognized the audible absence of the rocks, and caught himself a step before running into her.

Ava turned to face the direction they had come and steadied herself in an attempt to focus her ears. *It's something. No, it's nothing. You're hallucinating. Wait. No. Wait. It is something. Something mechanical, something with lights. I can see the lights.*

"Do you see it?" she asked him, and saw him transfixed on the yellow circles that grew larger and followed the shallow depressions and hills as it neared. "Yeah, you see it, Charlie."

The high beams threw sharp light on the small figures standing motionless alongside the road. Ava held her hand at her brows to redirect the light's focus, while Charlie was content to go blind. The automobile slowed; the high beams reverted to their lower, less intrusive counterparts. Ava dropped her hand to her side and, as her eyes adjusted, tried to make out the figure behind the wheel. It was only when the passenger door opened that she realized the uncertainty she had brought upon herself, and to Charlie.

Over her left shoulder was the ditch, and beyond that, the brush and thickets that come by man's intervention and eventual abandonment. A fence, broken where the rot had taken hold, each of these were suitable hiding places. The murderers would not ply their trade within the branches. The rapists, the lustful men who would touch a young girl like her, down *there*, would not be lurking among the hares and slumbering does. Yet, as the shadowy figure set a foot to the pavement, there was left only hope. Hope that empathy and decency would emerge and deliver them to shelter—to some understanding of the last days that had transpired.

"Sweet, sweet child," the woman said, knelt in front of Ava. "My sweet, sweet child." Her skin was taut about her face, which made her bones more prevalent and her eyes a prominent feature that could not be ignored. They searched about Ava's presence. Her demeanor, her expressions as they adjusted to the moment, how she stood. At first, the eyes made Ava uncomfortable, as if she was being analyzed in some animalistic way, but when the woman put her hand on her shoulder, she found warmth and kindness within those eyes.

"What's your name," the woman asked. "What's your name, sweet child?"

Ava cleared her throat. "Ava."

"Such a pretty name. Are you lost?"

"Yes"—Ava paused—"ma'am."

"Have you been hurt?"

Ava's mind pushed her to exclaim, loudly: the plane crash, her mother's death, the man in the woods. "No, ma'am."

The woman smiled, let it linger, then stood and shifted her attention to Charlie, who craned his neck to see her face at such a height. "And your name," she started, and then knelt before him, "what's your name, child?"

Charlie kept his gaze on her face until the wind ruffled the soft white cotton of her dress. He reached out slowly, cautiously, and traced the rose imprints along her arm.

"His name is Charlie," Ava said quietly.

"Charlie," she said, matching Ava's volume, "that's a wonderful name." Ava smiled broadly, having named him. She let him feel the fabric and, in return, she ran her fingertip and thumb along a length of the leash.

"Are you hungry, Charlie?"

He released her arm and surveyed the light and dark of their surroundings. "Thirs," he said. She smiled, and awaited more context.

"He's thirsty," Ava explained, when no context came.

The woman stood. "Come, children." And she walked assuredly towards the car. When she didn't sense footfalls behind her, she stopped and turned her bony neck back. "Come, children," she repeated, motherly. Ava stood still, and when the woman stared and did not direct them again, she took the first of the steps towards the car.

***

The man in the driver's seat pulled down on the shifter and pushed slowly on the gas pedal. He drove out from the gravel shoulder and gripped the steering wheel tightly with both hands. "That's good," he stated with a high octave, as a man does when conversing with children. "Back on the road, get the speed up to fifty-five, no more, and straight on for …" He paused. "Dear, how many miles are we to go straight?"

"Four and a half, considering that we stopped about a half mile before the next mile."

"Thank you, dear."

He wore a dress hat and a suit, which fit loose on his shoulders.

"Okay," Charlie said, without a prompt.

"It is okay," the man said. "Soon, your thirst will be quenched and your hunger abated."

"It is okay," the woman confirmed.

"Yes, dear."

"Okay," Charlie added, to end the conversation.

Ava stared out the window in the back seat and wondered. *Why had they stopped? Why hadn't she asked where they had come from? Where they were from? Maybe she just saw two young kids alone in the night and figured she'd get us somewhere safe and then ask those questions. Yes, those questions will come. We are safe. At least, I think we are safe.*

"Three miles, still."

"Three miles," the woman repeated, then pulled down the maroon visor and exposed the mirror. Ava spied where perfect curls rolled up at the ends of her hair, and watched her apply a thick layer of lipstick. The small, rectangular lights made the woman's wrinkles plain. *She's older than mom, probably fifty or maybe sixty. Older than mom was.*

"Steady, Michael," the man said, as a semi-truck approached and illuminated the entirety of the cabin. Ava slid into the center seat and saw his wrinkles too. His round, stubbled cheeks, the gray and white whiskers. The milky paleness of his hands as he gripped the vinyl steering wheel.

"You are steady, Michael," the woman assured him, and the man closed his eyes momentarily when the truck rumbled past the sedan. When it was gone, Michael released an extended exhale.

"Two miles, that is all."

"You are doing wonderful."

Ava turned her head, and stared at the red taillights of the truck until they became imperceptible. Fate, at her age, was yet to be an understandable concept, only a vague ideal thrown haphazardly under playground slides and ventured by overeager teachers. Her choice to stand at the road's edge was her choice. To enter this car, also hers. When the red lights disappeared, so did the choices she did not make, for they did not hide, and they were not in the cab of that truck.

"Steady, Michael," the man said again, and Ava spun her head back.

"You are steady, dear." The woman put her hand on Michael's knee as he slowed at the approaching stop sign. "Well done." When the brakes squeaked and held.

"A right turn," Michael announced. "That's it, fine, fine in the turning and no automobiles along this steady road."

"One mile, dear."

"Thirs," Charlie reminded.

"Yes, child, soon."

"Where are we going?" Ava asked meekly.

The woman leaned her head over the front seat and smiled with her newly glossed lips. "Home, Ava. We are going home."

"Who's home?"

"Our home."

"Steady. Steady." And Michael pulled off the road and up a windy dirt driveway enclosed in old trees that resembled a tunnel in the dark. "Twenty seconds." The trees ended, and the car entered a large clearing.

Ava sat up and followed the high beams. A short wooden fence. A picnic table at the edge of a pond. Flowers set in rectangular boxes that ran along the base of the house. The white front door set against the darker color of the house and a wooden porch swing. The car lights shut off and Michael exhaled.

"Wonderful, dear," the woman complimented, and only once the engine sputtered off did Michael release his grip from the wheel.

"We are home," he said.

"Yes, dear. Yes, children. We are home."

Charlie sat forwards and stared at the porch swing half lit by a single light. He spoke three, jumbled syllables, then quickly exited the back seat.

"Charlie!" Ava yelled, then chased after him. He sat down on the porch swing and pushed himself forwards with the balls of his feet. A smile crested upon his lips, he rubbed his hands together, and squealed.

"You like that, huh?" Ava asked, then sat down next to him and swung in unison. "I like these too."

Michael and the woman watched the children from the car. The back door was still open, and the cabin light lit their faces.

"Did I do good?" Michael asked the woman.

"Yes, dear," she responded.

"We have a family. I have given you children."

"No, dear. You have given me *a* child."

10

The wood floor creaked from behind the bathroom door. The woman unlatched the lock, and Charlie stood shivering in the doorway, lit dimly by a yellowed bulb set in a sconce on the hallway wall. An olive-green bath towel hung from his neck, and he held it tightly against his torso.

Ava stood near, motionless, holding her own olive-green towel. She watched the woman take Charlie by the hand, lead him into a bedroom, and close the door. She listened to the creaks and imagined the innocuous and the vile occurring beyond her sight. Strained to hear anything audible from below on the main floor of the house, where she had last seen Michael. Nothing was audible in the still of night, save the creaks beyond the door shut tight.

She heard steps draw closer, and the door swung open. Charlie stepped into the hallway, and Ava giggled when she saw him. He wore a white, button-down dress shirt and brown slacks that were worn at the knees—each two sizes too small for his frame.

The woman scowled, and Ava reverted back to a neutral expression. "Please, dear Ava," the woman urged, and extended her arm towards the bathroom door. Ava hesitated, and the woman forced a smile. Slowly, Ava walked into the bathroom, aware of every groan her steps made on the old wood. She looked back to see Charlie slink down onto the floor, and then, the door closed.

"What's your name?" Ava asked, demurely. The woman reached her hand into the dirty bathwater and pulled the plug. The water gurgled, then whirlpool down into the hidden pipe. The light, as in the hallway, was dim. A lime-green dress with a strip of white along the bottom hung from a hook.

"You may call me, 'Miss Delilah.'"

"Miss Delilah," Ava said aloud, "that's a pretty name."

"It is not for you to determine beauty in such things."

Ava, not knowing how to respond to the statement, stepped backwards until her back touched the farthest wall from the woman.

Miss Delilah reset the plug, and the tub filled with water. She placed a white bar of soap along the edge of the porcelain. Next to it, a green bottle of shampoo. She turned the faucet and waited until the droplets concluded. With a parting glance at Ava, she left the bathroom and shut the door tight.

Ava cautiously stepped from the wall and set the towel on the sink fringe. There was denial written about her face as she stared into the mirror. The dirt smudged across her face was not real. The dirt embedded in her clothing and under her fingernails were mere hallucinations, and if she closed her eyes tight enough-and for long enough, she would awaken. The jet would continue its journey through the clouds. Charlie would return to his sapped mother—or to an alternate universe. The man would stay hidden in the pines. If she closed her eyes with all her might.

The dirt fled her skin, and floated in the tepid water. She lifted her arm from under the surface and listened to the echoes as the beads fell from her fingertips. Held her breath and sunk her head. Squeezed the shampoo into her palm and lathered it into her hair. Submerged, and the suds mingled with the dirt. Rubbed the bar of soap against her skin, and drove the slippery bubbles into her cheeks, her forehead. Submerged, stood, and wrapped herself into the towel.

"Everything," Ava whispered into the mirror, "everything will be okay. Charlie will be okay. *I* will be okay. Mom will be okay." She dried herself, set the towel at the edge of the tub, and slipped on the green dress with its white fringe. "No, mother is dead. *I* am mother now. Mother to Charlie."

Miss Delilah pushed open the bathroom door, and only Ava's eyes adjusted to watch her in the mirror. She approached the young girl, stood behind her, and ran a brush through her wet, tangled hair. Ava stared ahead, into the mirror, watching the brush get stuck in the chestnut knots. Ava watched a tear, then another, as Miss Delilah yanked through the tangles.

"There is no beauty without pain," Miss Delilah said flatly, and brushed until Ava's hair lay flat against her neck.

***

Michael sat at the head of the dining room table, his left hand atop his right, set in his lap. Charlie, next to him, watched as Miss Delilah led Ava to her seat.

She perceived the quiet here acutely, every sound accentuated and echoed, as in the bathroom. There was formality, the way Michael sat at attention. The perfect arrangement of the plates, the cutlery. As Ava looked around furtively, she noticed that there was nothing that *could* make a sound. No television, no telephone, no radio, no clock. This was a house to be forgotten, to have no memory. It was if they were still adrift in the infinite woods, each tree indistinct, and providing no reference.

Charlie reached for the glass of water set out before him, and as he lifted, Miss Delilah slammed her palm down on the table. He stared at her, glass aloft. "Okay?"

She seethed.

"Okay?"

Ava gently took the glass from his grasp, set it down, and took his hand into hers under the table. Michael turned his head to Miss Delilah and waited while the children watched.

"Now," Miss Delilah said softly.

Ava handed the glass to Charlie. "It's okay," she told him when he hesitated. From there, she gingerly placed the roasted meat on his plate. The green beans, and a slice of bread. He drank quickly, awkwardly, and the water dribbled down his chin.

Miss Delilah watched him. Ava watched her watch him, and she refilled his glass from the plastic pitcher. Miss Delilah watched how he ate, and Michael watched her watch him. How the brown juices fell as he chewed with his mouth open, soiling his white shirt.

Ava watched Michael watch Miss Delilah, and there was a subtle, secretive conversation between the two adults. Thoughts were exchanged, and conclusions made. Although she didn't know what was discussed, it was in that moment that the hate swelled within her. It smoldered in her stomach, fumed in her chest, and coalesced in her eyes. *This woman, this, Miss Delilah, cannot be trusted. We must escape, or she must die.* And Ava blushed, having thought of a deed in which she had no capacity to follow through.

The click of forks. Knives press against the meat, scraping the plates below. Charlie's sparse teeth gnashing, flush with saliva. Every sound was identifiable and distinct. Every audible moment highlighted, and with each new salvo, Ava wished for the man in the woods to push down the door. To enter the dining room, a superhero cape flowing behind him, and proclaim them his children. And she and Charlie would take refuge from Miss Delilah's eyes, behind the man's thick torso. Heroically, he would lead them out into the night, and in the dawn her world would make sense.

11

The bareness of the bedroom matched that of the house she had seen. A lamp, without a shade, threw a dusty, yellowed pall in the corner. Everything was old wood, and only in sections did the original stain still remain. Worn at the bedframe where legs had slid down to the floor. Disappeared from the dressing table from elbows and forearms. Gone from the chest, where rears had rested.

Ava adjusted the white nightgown so the neck would stop falling down her shoulder. She inspected the loose threads, and, used to T-shirts and shorts, tried to adjust to the foreign material.

She stood from the bed and stepped lightly towards the bedroom door. She put her heel to the floor, then gingerly brought down the ball of her foot. The creaks, though not gone, were dampened. She turned the doorknob and pulled lightly. With more force. With her might.

She pivoted, took the same precarious steps to the window, and looked down from the second story. The moonlight cast a blue radiance, and as her eyes acclimated, she could make out the automobile, the drive, and the pond.

Her hands pressed against the thick wire mesh that covered the window. As she pulled, felt the nails that drove the impediment into the wall, she realized that Charlie must be in his own bedroom. Locked in, imprisoned, and she took solace that he may be oblivious to his predicament.

Time had become philosophical, an unending cycle of light and darkness. The months and days lost their meaning. Clock faces became Dali's, melted and warped. Her physical fatigue clashed with her mental alertness. She lay on the bed, counted shadowy spiders she imagined clung to the ceiling, and drifted to sleep.

With her eyes closed, she was unsure if the noise was real, or in dream. A reverberating thud that repeated every few seconds. Her eyelids fluttered, opened, and she sat back against the headrest and listened.

It's not my door, but not far. This floor.

A door creaked open. *Thud.* A door closed. *Thud.*

A voice. Whose? That man's? I hate that man. No, wait. Charlie. And the man.

The banging stopped, and was replaced with clomping footfalls. Charlie wailed. The man said something. It was a flat tone, though too muffled for Ava to understand. A thud, this time louder, and Ava's bed shook. Charlie wailed.

"Okay!" Charlie yelled. Not in anger, but confusion. Ava's heart pumped hard, but she did not move.

"It's okay, Charlie," she whispered to herself.

A quiet interlude, then another *thud.* Silence. Three bangs in succession.

"Okay!" Charlie screamed, his voice muffled to Ava through the closed doors. "Okay." And his voice cracked. He kept repeating the word, and each time it lost its clarity more as his sobs rose.

Ava yanked on the doorknob, and set her feet to increase her strength. *Was it a simple act that would calm him? A glass of water, or an escort to the bathroom? Or was it the unfamiliarity that had upset him? The pines were, of course, different, yet the extreme difference could have made comparisons beyond his comprehension. That bedroom, which he must understand, was not his.*

Ava heard a door open, then shut. Steady steps on the stairs, and then uneven plods. Feet on stairs that faded until she heard the creak of a door below. She went quickly to the window, waited, and thought she could hear conversation—but was not sure.

Michael emerged through the front door first, and Ava watched him walk down the porch steps from the second-floor window. He stopped, turned back towards the door, and yanked on the leash. Charlie stumbled forwards, and once in motion, followed Michael.

She stared out, her eyes fixed. The two dark figures walked down the drive, past the automobile, and Michael led them into the reeds that lined the pond.

"No," Ava whispered.

Michael entered the water and pulled on the leash. Charlie followed calmly, and his legs disappeared into the pond.

"No," Ava repeated, louder. She dug her fingers into the metal mesh, but could not get a hold. Tried to pry the nails, but they were flush. She ran to the dressing table and searched the drawers for a tool, for anything, yet they were empty. She flung herself to the floor and inspected under the bed. In the closet, there were no hangars, only a chest of clothes.

She went back to the window, her fingernails dug into the mesh, and she stared down at the pond. Charlie was immersed to his chest, and he was looking up at Michael. She wondered if he was saying 'okay' to him. If what was happening was the man's doing or Miss Delilah's. *What was* happening.

"No!" Ava screamed as Michael's hand extended and pushed down on Charlie's head. She banged her fists against the mesh. "Stop! Stop!"

Michael tilted his head and watched Ava in the window. Charlie reached and grabbed the man's hand as his chin submerged.

Ava stepped back, then forwards with her foot extended. She kicked at the metal. Through sobs. Through screams meant to deter. And Michael watched her up in the window as he set his other arm on Charlie's head and put him under.

Time, here, in this moment, pulled itself together. It became structured in Ava's mind. She had, as most children, tested the limits of holding one's breath underwater. She knew her limit, and even if she could break through the window, or bust down the door, time would not deny the inevitable. She pressed her palms against the mesh and sniffled to end her tears.

Rage consumed her as Charlie's head remained below the surface. She imagined retribution, as she had the man in the woods. Considered the different avenues to success. A knife, a gun, a baseball bat. And as Michael raised Charlie's lifeless body from the pond, she remembered her young, weak body. The death she witnessed on the plane was distant, surreal. This was deeper, closer. She felt it as though there was no window, as if she was in the pond with them. *Yet her constitution,* she thought, *would not allow her to enact vengeance here.*

Numb with the new knowledge that there were things, evil things, that she could never stop, Ava slid onto the bed. She pulled her knees tight against her chest, and waited for the dawn.

12

Strings broke the morning silence. A violin, or a cello, Ava could not tell. She lay and listened. It was a pretty song, but she did not know it.

There were footsteps when the music ended. Across the floor below, up the stairs, and culminating at her door. A key unlocked the door, and the footsteps retreated. Ava stayed prone for several minutes, then stood slowly.

The kitchen smelled of eggs and bacon sizzling in a pan. A jar of sweet jam made Ava's mouth water. She sat down at a chair and stared at the one where Charlie was the night before.

"You have not changed," Miss Delilah said while tending to the pan. Ava studied the white nightgown. "You must be dressed for breakfast." Miss Delilah turned to her. "Your hair is acceptable, yet you will brush it after you have eaten. Do you understand?"

"Yes," Ava said, feebly.

"Tomorrow, you will be proper."

"Yes."

"Yes, what?"

"Yes, Miss Delilah."

Miss Delilah flashed a quick smile at Ava, then turned her attention to the pan.

"Where's Charlie?" Ava asked boldly.

Miss Delilah set her hands to the sides of the stove and bent slightly. "No, dear. That was no child of mine." She then prepared three plates with the bacon and eggs, and spread butter and jam neatly across the toasted bread.

Michael arrived and sat down at the table. Ava watched his movements, yet he took no notice of her. She imagined the butter knife—not sharp enough. The fork—it wouldn't go deep enough.

A plate was set in front of her, which caused her to swallow hard to brush away the guilt. Guilt that her hunger could supersede the death she had, only hours earlier, witnessed. Guilt that she was only feet from a murderer, and perhaps, the catalyst of said killer. Her senses, and primal drive, overrode any sense of vengeance. She sat, in silence, and waited for the collective silence that had preceded the previous meal. Miss Delilah sat down, gazed at each of them, and then bent her head towards the table. The silence. "Now," Miss Delilah said softly, and Ava cut into her eggs and tasted the sweet jam.

The grip on Ava's fork alternated. Tightened as a weapon directed, in her thoughts, at the murderer and his accomplice. Loosened, when she took another bite of the food provided by her current caretakers.

The weight of caring for Charlie had lifted, relieved her of an onus meant for someone older, someone more mature. Her mother, lifeless in the airplane cabin, had led her to a new mother—through God's will, or fate, or mere happenstance. A new father, however murderous.

She discerned the heat of embarrassment flush her cheeks at the selfish thoughts. Of how she found comfort in the dead as it benefited her. Her grip tightened on the fork, and then she set it down on the table.

"May I be excused?" Ava requested.

"To what end, child?" Miss Delilah asked.

"I need to use the restroom."

"'Bathroom,'" Miss Delilah corrected, "We are not at a truck stop."

"Yes, Miss Delilah, I need to use the bathroom."

"May I."

"May I use the bathroom?"

"Yes, dear. You may be excused."

Ava pushed her chair with her bare feet and stood. Miss Delilah watched her, then turned to Michael, and nodded. Ava paused, and as she and Miss Delilah watched Michael stand, she moved the handle of her fork into her palm. Gingerly, with her fingertips, she clasped the tines until they were hidden, and the handle pressed against the inside of her forearm.

Miss Delilah turned back and watched Ava push her chair into the table with an open palm and a fist. With Ava's first step, Miss Delilah reached out and grabbed her arm.

"Ava, dear," she said quietly. "Leave the fork."

Ava stood, frozen, flushed upon her cheeks. Miss Delilah released her grip, and Ava set the fork on the table.

"Your youth," she said softly to Ava, "leads you to unwise decisions. Remember that, dear. I cannot guide you if you give in to your base instincts. Do you understand?"

"Yes, Miss Delilah," she responded, meekly, not fully comprehending.

"Good." Miss Delilah's warm palm enveloped Ava's knuckles.

Ava waited for her hand to be released, then turned and walked down the hallway to the bathroom. She sensed Michael's presence behind her as she entered. He shut the door, a waft of air rushed past her, and she shuddered.

She tried to ascertain if he was waiting outside the door or had returned to the kitchen, yet he made no sound.

The first-floor bathroom was smaller than where she had bathed the night before—a toilet, hand towel, and a thin mirror above the sink with a peeling, faux-gold frame. Ava pulled up her nightgown and sat down on the toilet seat.

For several minutes, Ava sat and examined the cramped bathroom, which was much smaller than where she had bathed the night before. Cream wallpaper adorned with butterflies in flight; how it peeled where it met the ceiling. The white porcelain of the toilet and, above the pedestal sink, an aged mirror within a faux-gold frame. A yellowed bulb that hung from a decorative chain. A white towel slid through a silver hoop.

Michael cleared his throat from the other side of the door, which Ava heard. She took the towel that hung from the silver loop and wrapped it around her fist. After inspecting the wrap, she unraveled the fabric, then overlaid again—this time tighter. She threw a punch into the air, then another. *A knock.*

"I'm almost done, sir," Ava said through the door and rapid heartbeats.

"Our breakfast is going cold."

"Almost done."

Ava threw another punch, then stood up. She turned the hot and cold faucets fully open, then gauged the distance between the toilet handle and the mirror. Then, with a deep, deliberate inhale, pushed down on the lever to flush the toilet. At the first *whoosh* of water, she struck the mirror. The reflective fragments fell into the sink and onto the floor.

As the tank filled with water, Ava unwrapped the towel halfway, laid a large shard in her palm, then tightened the towel around the glass. She turned off the faucets with her free hand, and froze.

Vengeance, at this moment, was real. Everything flashed before her on the closed door, as if she was watching a film reel in school. Her father holding her. The day her mother told her they were moving. The hallucinatory experience as the plane crashed through the pines. How Charlie had been a stranger, and in an instant, a brother. The man in the woods and the taste of charred fox meat. The devil masquerading as a mother at the kitchen table, and her weak manservant who stood just beyond the door.

A knock. "Are you coming out?" Michael asked.

Ava closed her eyes. "For Charlie," she whispered, almost inaudibly. She set her hand on the knob, hesitated, then turned hard and flung the door open.

Michael brought to bear a smile, and, when he saw the intensity in her eyes, quickly withdrew it. He turned towards the kitchen, having not noticed that Ava's right hand was hidden behind her back. She followed, her bare feet sticking slightly to the bare wooden floor.

There was an opportunity to, she thought, *to simply run*. Run the opposite way down the hallway. Alleviate the intense pressure in her chest that was overcoming her, that was becoming unbearable. The guilt of attacking this man, of *sinning* monstrously deep. Yet, the opposing thought that *not* attacking, that too, was wrong. He had committed a murderous act on a child, a child that could not comprehend the idea of sin. Here, before her, was a sinner that required a response— and yet her hand remained concealed.

Michael halted halfway to the kitchen, spun towards Ava, and kneeled down in front of her so he was at her eye level.

"Dear," he said softly, "Ava," as he ran his hand through her hair. "It's better to accept her, not to fight."

He put his hand on her shoulder, and his fingers rubbed against her nightgown. "Now, let's go finish our wonderful breakfast that she's prepared."

Ava let his words linger. She lifted her hand and placed it on top of his. A true smile came to her lips involuntarily, and he reciprocated. As she squeezed his hand atop hers, she thrust the glass dagger into his neck.

She expected him to scream. Expected herself to run immediately. Neither happened. The shock of what had transpired froze him in place, save the smile that now displayed disbelief. She kept the shard pushed hard, transfixed by a deed that could not be undone.

Ava tilted her head as Michael struggled to comprehend the mortality set forth for him. Now, not in some future, either foreseen as the progression of cancer or the immediacy of an obscured bullet. And as she yanked the broken glass, she watched his blood gush from the vein onto the floor and the wall.

Michael's hand slipped from Ava's shoulder. She blinked for the first time since the glass pierced his skin, and lucidity returned. She set her feet and bolted for the front door. Turned the locks, turned the handle, and broke through the screen door.

She threw the shard into the drive and unwrapped the towel as she passed the car. She didn't feel the gravel digging into her bare feet as she ran. Past the pond, down the driveway. She remembered turning right when they arrived at the house, so she turned left at the road.

She ran. Down the middle of the pavement, she pounded over the yellow lines that divided the country highway. A pickup truck slowed down, blared its horn, then sped off.

A sedan approached and decelerated. "Are you okay, dear?" an elderly woman asked from the passenger seat. Ava turned and looked at her. "Are you okay, dear?" the woman repeated, louder.

Ava didn't see an old woman, she saw Miss Delilah, and that meant it *could be* Miss Delilah. *Dear. Dear* was death. It was anguish and vulnerability and helplessness. The word chased her down the road until she veered off. Into the gravel along the shoulder. Through the thick weeds and along the fence line of an old farm. Past the windbreak of tall trees that separated the fields and into the corn. Exhausted, she collapsed into the dirt between the stalks.

She rolled onto her back. Listened to the wind rustle the leaves of the corn, and watched the wispy clouds. Everything else faded, dissipated into the ether. She glimpsed the blood drying on the nightgown sleeve and down her arm. Her eyes closed, she forced them open, then succumbed to the exhaustion that had built up over the past days.

13

Ava woke in the midafternoon. Pulled her face from the ground, and wiped the dirt and twigs from her face and her arms. Felt dryness in her throat when she swallowed and the tip of her tongue pressed against the roof of her mouth. Rubbed the dried blood from her arm and cursed the stains on the nightgown.

She looked up, let the sun blind her, and let loose a shrieking scream into the sky. Satisfied with the release, she walked the row between the corn.

"I won't let anything happen to you," she whispered as she pulled open a husk. "I'll protect you," she told the corn cob. "From all the crazies in this world. Everything's going to be okay, Charlie."

She walked several feet, and peeled back another. "Everything will be okay. They will come. They will come and bring you back. Take you to your mom and she will hold you tight and take you to your bedroom and tuck you in. I have a purple comforter with white flowers. At least, I did have a purple comforter with white flowers. I don't have it anymore. I don't have much anymore."

Ava went to the next stalk. "I'm going to protect you, Charlie. I've seen the men with bad ideas in their eyes. I've seen the woman who would harm you just for who you are. Who would *kill* you." Ava's eyes closed, and she yanked the husk from the stalk. "I won't let them, Charlie. I won't let them."

She pulled the silk, strand by strand, from the husk. Each one, a loose, delicate thread. And when she heard the drone of a helicopter, distant, she did not waver from her task.

The real and the imagined had melded. She wavered on her survival, her very existence. Believed the man in the woods a mere hallucination. Charlie, her coping mechanism, had only existed as a coping mechanism—therefore he could not have been drowned in the pond.

She was not in a corn field. No, she was dead, burned alive on that airplane. Or, she had jumped, and was dead *next* to that airplane. This was that vivid dream that those who come back from death tell to the newspapers. That vivid dream that lasts days in the mind, yet could only last mere moments according to the doctors that revived them. At least, that's what they tell the news reporters who set up in clean, suburban living rooms.

Still, the helicopter grew louder. Ava twirled a silk between her thumb and forefinger, then let it fall. *A vivid dream,* she thought. *Just a vivid dream.*

What was a black spot on the horizon had taken shape. She lowered the husk to her side, and watched the helicopter as it neared. Saw its flat bottom and the blur of the rotors. It flew over the field. The wash pushed the corn down and ruffled the leaves. When it continued on, the rows rebounded, and Ava pulled another silk.

"I'm going to call you Charlie," Ava told the cob. "You look like a Charlie."

Sirens, maybe? I wonder if I'm a ghost.

A cacophony of sirens neared. Screeched, made the deer alert, the hares frightened, and drove Ava from the field to test her ghost theory.

She stood alongside the road, and tried to look eerie in the white nightgown, her tangled hair, and bare, dirty feet.

Two police cars sped past her first. Then the ambulances. *I am a ghost.* The fire trucks. *I am dead.*

The clamor diminished behind her, and the road went quiet. With her ghost theory confirmed,

Ava turned and walked alongside the road. A group of vans rushed past. Each with an antenna affixed to its roof. Slogans written in bold letters on the side panels and rear doors. 'Local News First.' 'First at Five.' 'Channel 2: At the Heart of it.'

"Boo!" Ava yelled as they accelerated after the ambulances and fire trucks. "I'm a ghost! Interview me!"

She walked after the vans. Slowly, with no intention of catching them. Another police car rushed down the road. No sirens, no flashing lights. She smiled as it passed, satisfied in her ghostly form.

A few hundred feet in front of her, the brake lights flipped on, and the cruiser pulled to the side of the road and stopped. The officer stepped out, and shut his door softly. He walked to the back of his car, rested his rear against the trunk, and watched Ava.

Her gait slowed, but she did not stop. At fifty feet, she noticed his height. At twenty, the officer bent at his knees to match her short stature. At ten, she saw his blond hair on his shoulders, mostly hidden by a mahogany cowboy hat. His youthful face, clean-shaven and taut. The gold star that glinted, pinned to his beige uniform. The gun, and the handcuffs.

At five feet, Ava watched his eyes searching for clues. Her mussed hair from sleeping in

the field. The blood stains on the nightgown—
how she was wearing a nightgown. Her dirty,
bare feet.

"Can you," she started. "Can you see me?"

He glanced down, picked up a handful of
pebbles, and threw them aside. "Yes, miss," he
responded, and looked up. "I can see you."

She was not expecting his drawl, how he
elongated the word 'you.' He waited for
another question, yet she asked none. "Are
you okay?"

"I was a ghost."

"Well"—he peeked at the fields, and then
back at her—"sometimes, we're in situations,
in places, where we feel like we're not seen."

"I really was."

"I believe you," he said, and put his arm on
her shoulder. "I'm Officer John, but you can
just call me 'Johnnie.' What's your name?"

Ava inspected his eyes. She had seen Miss
Delilah's eyes, and there, too, she had
determined trust. She was tired, sapped from
figuring out which adults were sincere, and
which had evil intent.

"Ava," she said softly, relinquishing herself
of the onus, of detecting intent on the faces of
elders.

"Ava," he repeated. "That's a pretty name."

"There was a devil that told me the exact
same thing."

"Excuse me?"

"Nothing."

Johnnie grabbed her wrist, and gently pulled her arm. "Who did this to you?"

Ava spied the dried blood still embedded in her skin, stained on the nightgown.

"Michael."

"Michael?" Johnnie questioned. "Is Michael your father?"

"No."

"But Michael did this?"

"No. Michael *made me* do this."

"What do you mean?"

Ava pulled her arm back, and Johnnie did not resist. She twirled the loose strings at the nightgown's hem. A straggling news van drove past.

"What took you so long?" she asked the officer.

"What?"

"What took you so long?"

"Well, a lot of times, in these situations, we're not aware that something's going on. So, it's a good thing I found you, right? This Michael won't hurt you anymore, and that's a promise."

"I'm the only one who survived."

"Survived what?"

"The plane."

Johnnie took a moment to process her declaration. He stood and turned towards the crash scene. The helicopter was a small black dot on the horizon, barely audible. He shifted back to her. The nightgown, the blood, and the bare feet.

"You took too long," she informed him flatly, "and Charlie is dead."

"Who's Charlie? Why are you all the way out here? Where's your shoes? Wait, then who's Michael?"

"Thirs."

"What?"

"I'm thirsty."

"I'll get you some water, but I'm trying to understand."

"If I'm not a ghost, then everything happened."

"What happened?"

Ava pulled her arm back, and took a step towards the officer. "You took too long." She tried to will the tears to stay hidden, yet failed. "What took you so long?"

Johnnie stared at her, and his expression shifted between comforting to confusion. "I don't know. They just said they knew where it was now. The plane. That someone called and said they know where it went down."

"The man in the woods," she reckoned.

"Who?"

"A good guy, mostly." Ava wiped the tears, and regained her composure.

"And who's a bad guy?" Johnnie asked.

"You know who."

"Michael."

"And you've met these guys? Recently?"

"My mother is dead. Charlie… is dead. I'm thirsty."

"Where are you from? Where do you live?"

"I'm thirsty."

Johnnie stood up, watched a pickup truck slow when the driver saw the police car, then sped away. He squinted to see the helicopter on the horizon. "Ava," he said, while still exploring the distance. "What do you want to do? Right now?"

She opened her mouth, but did not speak. Her mother had told her they were moving. Her teachers had told her what to do with her school days. What was to be done, what was expected, and when tasks were to be completed. The man in the woods led her and Charlie. Miss Delilah bathed her, dressed her, and commanded her.

"Anything you want. I just want you to make me a promise."

"What's that?"

"When we're done with whatever you want to do, you tell me everything. What happened on that plane. Charlie, Michael, the man in the woods—from start to finish. Everything you can remember."

He turned to her, and she nodded in agreement. "So, what do you want to do?"

Ava stood motionless, and waited. She did not want to spoil this rare opportunity.

"I want new clothes. They don't have to be new, just new to me. A tee and shorts and socks and shoes." She pulled on the nightgown. "I want to burn this. I want to watch it burn. I want a big glass of orange juice and pancakes. Blueberry pancakes. I want to sleep in a bed where I don't have to worry. About anything, at least for one night."

"Anything else?" Johnnie asked, when she paused to think.

"I want to run the siren. That's all."

Johnnie smiled, opened the passenger door, and Ava climbed into the police car. He got in, turned the key in the ignition, and drove them away from the ambulances, fire trucks, and the helicopter.

"This"—he pointed—"this is the switch for the siren."

Ava set her finger under the switch, hesitated, then flipped it up. The sirens blared, she covered her ears, and turned it off.

"Loud, ain't it?" Ava turned and watched Johnnie. "I like to scare people with it," he said, with a mischievous grin.

She chuckled, then rolled down the window. "Okay," she said out the window, to Charlie in the ethereal. To Charlie in heaven. "I'm gonna be okay, Mom. I'm gonna do good."

She pulled the seat lever, pushed back to recline, and listened as Johnnie spoke into the CB radio to a woman's voice. A lone girl found along the road. A plane crash survivor. Is she injured?

"Are you injured?" he asked Ava.

"No."

"Not injured. How is she not injured? I don't know, she just isn't. Bring her to the station. No, not to the station. Cracker Barrel. Why? Just trust me. Clothes, she needs clothes. She's naked? No, just needs clothes. Just bring her to the station. She needs pancakes. What the hell does that mean? I'll see you at Cracker Barrel."

The warm summer air blew through Ava's hair as the miles of pines and fields drifted past them in the cruiser. She closed her eyes and let the wind deal with the future. What happens next? Who would she live with? Where? Had she grieved for her mother, or would that come next? And Charlie?

She let the thoughts float away and imagined the next minutes and hours. She saw herself in a new tee and shorts, kicking the opposite booth with her new shoes. Eating blueberry pancakes and gulping down a tall glass of orange juice. Cleansed of the last few days and rid of the nightgown.

There were two police cars in the Cracker Barrel parking lot when Johnnie and Ava arrived. Ava stepped out of the cruiser and the woman with her own gold star and gun stepped towards her. Middle-aged, with a thick build that filled out her uniform. Her black hair pulled into a ponytail.

She inspected Ava, then gave Johnnie a subtle, approving nod.

"I'm Jennifer," the female officer said. "What's yours?"

"Ava."

"It's nice to meet you, Ava."

She extended her hand, and Ava took it. If Jennifer had never seen trauma in a child's eyes, she would have offered sanctuary. Told the young girl that she was safe now, that she would be protected. No one would ever hurt her ever again. Yet, the traumatized have been reassured with promises—of change, of compassion, of love—deluged with promises that meant nothing.

And so, when Officer Jennifer asked plainly, "What kind of pancakes do you want?" Ava knew it was over, that she was safe.

Other books by Steven William Simon

Into the Fracking Fields

The kids in the border town watch the prisoners get off the trains and load up on the bus. Alice has heard the rumors of the people who stayed, their proximity to Nuclear One, their cancerous lumps. Her friend Carmen is driven to see the fracking pad where his father was killed – and Michael, unfortunately, is the only one that can get them there.

Red as Apple

It has been years since Keenan had been to the farm. He had vowed to move on, to move up, but this has brought him back. To his introverted older brother and confident sister. After this, their lives will never be the same.

1200 Miles from Los Angeles

When his car breaks down on his way to Los Angeles, Sanford takes a job at a small-town diner along the interstate to earn the money he needs to keep going west. He learns that his religion means something different there - for better or worse.

Out Pondered the Hare | Poems

A collection of poems written in sobriety. Or a Lorazepam fog. A whiskey-infused detour and lysergic-stamped synapses. All in the hopes that some of this makes sense to those who were not there in those specific instances where there is truth.

stevensimonbooks.com